THE ROARING RIVER MYSTERY

THE ROARING RIVER MYSTERY

Franklin W. Dixon

Illustrated by Paul Frame

WANDERER BOOKS

Published by Simon & Schuster, Inc., New York

Manufactured in the United States of America
10 9 8 7 6 5 4 3
10 9 8 7 6 5 4   pbk
THE HARDY BOYS, WANDERER and colophon
are registered trademarks of Simon & Schuster, Inc.

Library of Congress Cataloging in Publication Data
Dixon, Franklin W.
The roaring river mystery.

(The Hardy boys mystery stories; 80)
Summary: The Hardy brothers are involved in a mystery
that links whitewater rafting in Maine with a bank
robbery in Washington, D.C.
[1. Mystery and detective stories]   I. Frame, Paul, ill.
II. Title.   III. Series.
PZ7.D644Ro 1984   [Fic]   83-16927
ISBN 0-671-49722-7
ISBN 0-671-49721-9 (pbk.)

Contents

1 Life Savers!

Blond, seventeen-year-old Joe Hardy dipped his paddle into the water with a strong backward thrust, propelling their canoe forward along the shore of Lake Algonquin.

"This is great!" he said. "We have the whole lake to ourselves."

"Not quite," his older brother Frank replied. He pointed to a boat that was being skillfully handled by a youth their own age. It had just come into view and was heading away from the shore toward the center of the lake.

Then Frank did a double take. "Hey, Joe! This guy's being followed by two men in another canoe, and they're wearing ski masks! Do you see them?"

Joe squinted against the sun and nodded. "Looks like he's in trouble. Let's head over to him. Maybe we can help!"

The Hardys propelled their craft forward as fast as they could toward the young man, who was apparently unaware of his pursuers. Suddenly he heard the sound of the other boat behind him and whirled around. His eyes widened as he saw the two men almost upon him now. Frantically he tried to push them off with his paddle.

"He hasn't got a chance!" Joe cried.

Frank nodded as the masked men kept ramming the young man's canoe. It finally capsized, throwing its passenger into the water.

In a flash, the two masked men leaped in on top of him. One curled an arm around his neck and the other tore open the cords of his life jacket.

Frank and Joe paddled desperately. When they reached the spot where the struggle was raging, Frank jumped in on top of the man who had just torn off the youth's life jacket. Joe plunged in on the other attacker, and the surface of the lake churned into white froth as a battle royal erupted.

Joe was getting a hammerlock on his antagonist when he heard a cry for help. The boy

was going under! Quickly Joe released the masked man, swam to the youth, and pulled him up. He hooked a hand under his chin and towed him to the Hardys' canoe. The victim gasped and choked as Joe tried to push him into the craft.

Frank was still involved in a wrestling match in the water. Suddenly the man he had seized wrenched loose, pushed the life jacket in Frank's face, and swam after his confederate toward shore.

Frank was about to give chase, when he realized that Joe could not handle the choking youth alone. Quickly the older Hardy came to his help, and together they managed to push the young man into the canoe. Then Joe climbed in and Frank swam after the two men.

The young detective was a strong swimmer, but the men reached the shore way ahead of him. They clambered out of the water and ran toward a clump of pine trees. By the time Frank had scrambled out of the lake in pursuit, he could see neither of them. However, he heard them running through the underbrush.

He raced in the direction of the noise until he came to a clearing. One of the masked men was already behind the wheel of a parked car, the other was climbing in on the passenger side. Before Frank could prevent them, they careened off in a burst of speed and a cloud of dust.

Disconsolately, the boy watched the car roar through the underbrush to a dirt road and made a mental note of the license-plate number. A moment later, the car was out of sight altogether.

Frank returned to the lake and swam back toward his canoe. He saw the life jacket floating in the water, grabbed it, and pushed it ahead of him. As he did, he noticed a tear behind one of the cork panels. It was mended with a leather thread.

Frank threw the life jacket into the canoe, then Joe helped him aboard.

The young man was lying on the bottom of the canoe.

"Is he all right?" Frank asked.

"He swallowed an awful lot of water," Joe replied. "But he coughed up most of it. He'll be okay in a little while."

"You stay with him," Frank said. "I'll get the other canoes."

The two boats were slowly drifting away. Frank swam over to the capsized one, turned it over, threw in the paddle, and fastened the boat to their own craft. Then he went after the other canoe and tied it to the first one.

When he was done, he climbed aboard.

The stranger had gradually regained his breath and sat up. "Where am I?" he asked weakly.

Frank and Joe introduced themselves and explained what had happened. "Who are you?" Frank asked when they had finished.

"I'm Ollie Fernandez," the youth replied. "I live not far from here."

"Do you know who those men were?" Joe asked.

Ollie shook his head. "I couldn't see their faces through the masks."

"Do you know why they came after you?"

"I have no idea."

"Well," Frank said, "they pulled your life jacket off. Obviously they wanted to drown you."

"Try to figure out who they could be," Joe added.

Ollie frowned and said nothing for a few moments. Then he shrugged. "It's no use. I can't think of anybody."

He placed his hand against his forehead and began to shiver.

"We'd better get you home," Joe said. "Did you rent your boat at the marina?"

Ollie nodded.

"So did we. Just sit tight and we'll bring you

in. You're too weak to paddle your own boat."

Towing the two empty canoes, Frank and Joe paddled across the lake to a sign that read BOB MOORE'S MARINA. A number of boats were rocking in the water near the dock, and fishing poles stood in a rack along the side of the building. Nets were drying in the sun.

The boys tied the canoes to the dock. Joe and Ollie went into the office, while Frank used the outside phone to alert the local police to the car the masked men had escaped in. The sergeant on duty was unable to identify it, but he said he would warn his men to be on the lookout for the vehicle. Then Frank went inside and joined the others.

Joe and Ollie were talking to Bob Moore, a stocky man with a rugged face weather-beaten by years of deep-sea fishing. The boys paid for the two canoes they had rented. Frank mentioned the third canoe and explained how they had got it. Moore accompanied them out to the dock and looked at the craft.

"I'm grateful to you for bringing it back," he told them. "It was stolen from the marina last night!"

2 *The Roaring River*

"Do you suspect anyone?" Joe asked eagerly.

The man shrugged. "No. People are pretty honest around here. This is the first time it ever happened."

He mopped his brow with a large handkerchief, then said grimly, "I'd better keep an eye on my boats from now on."

"If you spot anyone suspicious, let us know," Frank said. "We're Frank and Joe Hardy, amateur detectives from Bayport." He gave the marina owner their telephone number, then said goodbye.

Ollie was too weak to drive his own car, so Joe offered to take him home. "You'll need

14

someone to look after you for a while," Joe said.

Ollie grinned ruefully. "My parents are away this week," he said. "I'm taking care of myself."

"Then you'd better come home with us," Frank suggested. "You can stay overnight if you want to."

Ollie looked relieved. "Thanks for the invitation," he said. "I'm not about to say no."

The boys showered and changed into dry clothes in the marina bathhouse, then Joe and Ollie drove to Bayport in the Hardys' yellow sports sedan. Frank followed in Ollie's car.

When they arrived at the Hardy home, Mrs. Hardy opened the door for them. She was an attractive, slim woman with a big smile on her face. "I saw you from the window," she said. "Actually, I didn't expect you back so soon."

"Our canoe ride was interrupted, Mother," Joe said. "We met Ollie here, and—"

"Why don't you come into the living room and tell me all about it," Mrs. Hardy suggested and led the way inside.

When the boys had finished their story, Mrs. Hardy looked worried. "I hope those masked men didn't follow you here," she said.

"We kept our eyes peeled in case they tailed us from the marina," Joe assured her. "But they weren't there."

"The last I saw of them, they drove away from the lake in the opposite direction," Frank said. "Which reminds me, I'd better report the incident to Chief Collig of the Bayport police. He may be able to trace that car."

Chief Collig was an old friend of the Hardy family and had often cooperated with the boys in their detective work.

"Glad to hear from you, Frank," the chief said when he picked up the phone. "What can I do for you?"

Frank told him what happened and gave him the license number of the getaway car. Chief Collig asked him to hold on while he checked. A few moments later, he came back on the line.

"You were right to call me, Frank. That car was stolen. But there's no use looking for it."

"Why not?"

"It was just found by one of our patrols. It was abandoned in a back alley in Bayport a little while ago. The motor was still warm."

"In Bayport?" Frank was worried. "That means either the crooks followed us after all, or they just happened to leave the car here. Either way, I don't like it."

"I'll have my men check out the car thoroughly," Chief Collig promised. "If we find

16

anything, I'll let you know. And be careful, will you?"

"We will," Frank said and hung up.

He returned to the living room just as Fenton Hardy's sister, Gertrude, was coming in from the kitchen to hear Joe describe the struggle in the water.

"That's Frank and Joe for you!" Gertrude Hardy said tartly. "Wherever they go, they run into criminals! Even in a canoe on Lake Algonquin! Two masked men! Well, I never!"

"They dropped the stolen car in Bayport," Frank said. "I wonder if they know where we are."

"You should stay home," Aunt Gertrude advised. "Your mother and I are going shopping, but I'd feel better if you boys didn't leave the house."

"We don't intend to," Frank assured her, and the two women left.

The boys went into the kitchen to get a snack, and afterward Ollie informed his new friends that he felt much better.

"It's a good thing, too," he said. "I'll have to be on my way north tomorrow."

"Where are you going?" Frank wanted to know.

"To the Roaring River," Ollie replied.

"That's up in Maine, isn't it?" Joe interjected. "It's part of the Allagash Wilderness Waterway. We've done a lot of backpacking in that area. But we never saw the Roaring River. We just heard about it from one of the Waterway Rangers."

"Most people don't know about it," Ollie said. "It's a small stream near the Canadian border. The rapids are the worst in the whole Allagash Wilderness Waterway, though. Like a series of waterfalls. You can hear the water hitting the boulders before you ever see the stream. That's how the Roaring River got its name."

"What are you going to do up there?" Frank inquired.

Ollie chuckled. "I heard that the state of Maine is offering a prize to the first expedition to run the Roaring River. I went and had a look at it, because I've done a great deal of white-water rafting. Nothing quite as challenging, though. Anyway, I've decided to try it!"

"You mean you're organizing a rafting expedition?" Joe cried out. "That's fantastic!"

"It's already organized," Ollie replied. "In fact, the other members of my crew are there now, in a cabin in the woods. We've been practicing our runs and testing our equipment, but I had to come home for a couple of days because the bank wanted me to sign some checks to pay for the expedition. Actually, I can't wait to get back."

"In that case, what were you doing out on Lake Algonquin?" Frank asked.

"A friend of mine, who's a private pilot, flew me home, but he's tied up with a client till tomorrow," Ollie said. "I knew I'd have today off, so I decided to get in some practice, and I always wear my life jacket when I'm alone on the water."

"I suppose you had to register with the Maine authorities," Joe said. "When we ran the rapids of the Allagash, we had to sign up with the Waterway Rangers."

"Oh, you know white-water rafting, too?" Ollie asked.

"Yes, we've done quite a bit of that."

Ollie nodded. "Yes, I had to register all the crew members. The rangers won't let us make the run till everything's ready. Actually, we're almost ready, except for one thing."

"What's that?" Joe wanted to know.

"Somebody's trying to stop us!"

3 Chet's Brainwave

The Hardys were startled by Ollie's revelation. Frank started to question him, but was interrupted by loud noises coming from the street. The banging and clanging sounds came closer.

"What's that?" Ollie exclaimed.

Frank laughed. "Don't worry. It's a car; it belongs to our friend Chet Morton. He's probably coming here."

"If you can call it a car," Joe quipped as he got up to look out the window. "It's a pile of loose bolts and blown gaskets that gives you a backache if you ride in it."

Chet Morton, a roly-poly youth, lived on a farm near Bayport. He took part in many of the

Hardys' adventures, and even though he preferred food to work, he could usually be relied
on when the young detectives needed help.

Chet pulled up in front of the house and
turned off the motor. The racket stopped, and
he jumped out of the car with a pleased expression on his face.

Frank met him at the door. "One thing about
you, Chet. You never sneak up on us. We could
tell you were coming a mile away!"

Chet grinned. "Guess what!"

"You're finally taking your jalopy to the junk-
yard," Frank said, pretending to be serious.
"You'll have it recycled for scrap."

Chet looked pained. "You're talking about
the best car in Bayport, Frank. It can get you
anywhere!"

"It nearly got me into traction last month."

By this time the two boys had walked into the
living room. "What's on your mind, Chet?" Joe
greeted him.

Chet drew a paperback book out of his pocket
and held it up. It was titled *Running the River
Rapids*. "I'm on my way to becoming the best
white-water rafter in town!" Chet crowed. "All
I need is a raft to put all my knowledge to use!"

The Hardys and Ollie broke out laughing.

"What's so funny?" Chet demanded.

"Meet Ollie Fernandez," Joe introduced his guest to his old friend. "He's an expert on the subject. Matter of fact, he's about to run an expedition down the Roaring River in Maine."

Chet looked a little embarrassed. "Oh. So, you know all about white water," he said to Ollie.

"You can never know enough," Ollie consoled him. "There are plenty of rivers to run, and no two are alike."

Chet brightened. "Tell me about your expedition," he said.

"We're almost ready to go, but as I was mentioning to the Hardys, someone's trying to stop us."

"How?" Chet wanted to know.

"By stealing out life jackets! The funny part is, they weren't taken all at once. They've disappeared from the cabin one or two at a time. Five from one shipment, and none of them is worth much. You can buy them in many stores. So the only thing we can think of is sabotage!"

"Wait a minute!" Frank said. "If someone wants your life jackets, maybe those two masked men didn't mean to drown you in the lake today. Maybe they were after your life vest!"

"What masked men and what lake?" Chet spoke up.

The boys quickly brought him up to date on the day's events, then Chet summed it up.

"So, you figure the motive is sabotage, Ollie? Someone wants you to go back home and not run the river. Is that it?"

"What else can it be?" Ollie replied.

Frank shook his head. "But if it's sabotage, why didn't the thief ransack the cabin and take everything he could carry? Losing five life jackets won't stop your expedition, will it?"

"No, I've ordered more. We're sticking to our schedule," Ollie declared.

"You see," Frank pressed the point. "There has to be more to it than sabotage. Is there anyone else near your cabin?"

"Yes. There's a rival expedition on the other side of the river," Ollie said. "We're competing to see who runs the rapids faster and wins the prize. Brian Schmidt's the leader of that group. He'll pull out all the stops to beat us!"

"He sounds like the one to talk to," Joe said. "Maybe he knows what's going on."

"Only he won't tell us if he's behind all of this," Frank pointed out.

Ollie nodded. "Anyway, we're watching our life jackets now. Whether it's Brian Schmidt, or somebody else, no one's going to steal any more from us! But I do have another problem. I'm three men short. The three who were supposed to ride the raft with me can't make it. I'm trying to train my maintenance men. I just hope they can learn fast enough!"

Chet broke out in a big grin. "Ollie, you're looking at three terrific river runners. The Hardys and me! We'll come with you. Right, Frank? Right, Joe?"

"That would be great!" Ollie exclaimed. "Besides, Frank and Joe are detectives. I heard them tell the marina owner." He turned to Frank. "Could you come up and investigate this mystery while training to be on my crew?"

Frank and Joe looked at one another. They liked the idea but said nothing.

Chet knew what that meant. "You have to wait to hear from your father, don't you? He's away on a case, and he may want you to take a hand in it."

Joe nodded. "We can't leave Bayport till he calls. He's in Washington on an investigation for the government. That's all we know."

The four boys began to discuss the Allagash Wilderness Waterway. Ollie pulled a map from his pocket and laid it on the table. They saw how the waterway extended for ninety miles, from Telos Lake in the south to West Twin Brook in the north. Ribbons of water connected

24

a series of large lakes in between, and numerous streams flowed into them from east and west.

"We ran the Chase Rapids in a canoe," Frank commented. "Nine miles of tough going. The only worse stretch we saw was the Allagash Falls. A forty-degree drop. We had to portage—get out of the river and carry our canoe around the falls before we could begin boating again. If we'd gone over the edge, the canoe would have been matchwood."

"And the rangers would still be looking for us at the bottom of the falls," Joe added.

Chet shivered. "Let's stay away from the Allagash Falls, fellows!" he pleaded.

"We'll be way north of the falls, Chet," said Ollie. "But it'll still be a hairy run. The Roaring River may be short, but the rapids are worse than the Chase Rapids for about a mile. It takes a rubber raft to make the run—if it can be done."

Suddenly the phone rang. Frank answered. He heard the tense voice of Fenton Hardy on the other end.

"I want you and Joe down here in Washington right away!"

4   *Top Secret*

"What's going on, Dad?" Frank asked excitedly, brushing a strand of dark hair from his forehead.

"I can't talk about it over the phone," his father replied. "But I need help. That's why I want you boys to catch the morning flight out of Bayport. Come to the Grandison Hotel. It's in the east section of Washington near the Union Station. I'll be waiting for you. Ask for Mr. Harper. Now, is there anything you want to tell me before I hang up?"

Frank mentioned Ollie Fernandez and his Roaring River expedition. He explained the mystery of the life jackets and how they had rescued Ollie on Lake Algonquin. "Ollie would like us to investigate," he concluded.

"Maybe you can still do that when we're finished here in Washington," Mr. Hardy replied. "Is your mother there? She's out shopping? Well, I'll phone her tonight."

Fenton Hardy hung up. Frank reported to the others what his father had told him.

Ollie's face fell. "I was hoping you could fly to Maine with me tomorrow," he said glumly. "But the race isn't until a week from now. Maybe you'll still be able to make it."

"Can we call you up there?" Frank asked.

Ollie shook his head. "The cabin doesn't have a phone. And there's nobody for miles around."

"Then we'll just come straight up. By the way, what kind of raft do you have?"

"It's twelve feet long and carries four people," Ollie replied. "The lookout is in front. The one who steers is in the rear, as you know, and the two others are on the oars in the middle. I'm one of the oars. If you join me, you three can divide up the other places among you."

"I'll take the second oar," Chet declared.

"How about the lookout for me?" Joe said.

"Good. That leaves me to steer the raft," Frank agreed.

"Thanks, fellows," Ollie said. "Right now I

have four maintenance men who take care of the raft and the canoes we brought to the cabin. We use canoes on the upper part of the river where we can explore the current and chart the best course. We need to know what the dangers are before we go downstream toward the rapids. If we don't do that, we're liable to hit a boulder we didn't know was there."

"Do you wear helmets and life jackets?" Chet asked.

"Always."

"I noticed there was a tear in your life vest when I fished it out of the water," Frank pointed out.

"I know," Ollie said. "It came that way from the store. Since the tear was so small, I figured it wasn't worth returning the jacket, so I mended it, and it works just fine."

"If we can join you," Joe spoke up, "how do we find the cabin?"

"Fly to an airstrip east of the Roaring River. You'll see a trail leading west. Stay on that and you'll come to our place. It's right on the river."

Chet got to his feet and stretched. "I'll wait for Frank and Joe and we'll all come up together. Now I'm going home. I have to study my book." He waved his copy of *Running the River Rapids*.

Ollie stood up, too. "I'm much better now," he said, "so I think I'll run along, too. Thanks again for saving me on the lake!"

"I'm glad we were there," Frank said. "It's just too bad the two men got away."

Ollie and Chet went outside, where Ollie backed his car out of the driveway and zipped away. Chet got into his jalopy and stepped on the gas. With a clanging noise, he rocked off along the street toward the Morton farm.

Frank and Joe spent the rest of the day reading about the Allagash Wilderness Waterway. Early the next morning, they drove to the airport, parked their car, and boarded their flight to Washington.

Two hours later, they stood in front of the reception desk at the Grandison Hotel. "We'd like to see Mr. Harper," Frank said to the clerk.

"Number 22. Second floor, third door on the right," the man replied. He eyed the Hardys suspiciously.

Frank and Joe walked up the stairs. When they arrived on the second floor, Frank suddenly pulled Joe behind a vending machine holding cookies and chocolate bars.

"What's the matter?" Joe whispered.

"I have a feeling the clerk is following us," Frank said in a low voice.

Sure enough, they heard footsteps coming up the stairs. The desk clerk appeared and moved stealthily down the hall toward the third door on the right.

Frank and Joe stepped from behind the machine and confronted him. "Are you going to Mr. Harper's room?" Frank asked innocently.

"Ah, that's right. I have a message for him," the clerk said with some hesitation.

"One too important to phone?" Frank asked. "Then why don't you come with us?"

The clerk looked uncomfortable, but made no objection and walked to room 22 with the Hardys on either side of him. Frank knocked on the door, carefully spacing the sounds. Three knocks, then two, and finally one. It was a code Fenton Hardy and his sons used in cases like this.

Mr. Hardy opened the door. He was surprised to see the desk clerk accompanying his sons.

"He was following us," Frank explained. "We figured we'd better find out why."

Mr. Hardy chuckled. "Ken, you're no match for these detectives," he said to the clerk. "I should have warned you."

The clerk shrugged. "You told me Frank and Joe Hardy would come to the hotel, but I thought they'd be a lot older. So when these two fellows arrived, I followed them in case they were up to something. Guess I got caught!"

"You did. Ken, meet my sons. Frank and Joe, this is Ken Bulow. He screens everybody who comes in. Which reminds me, Ken, you'd better get back downstairs. We need you to watch the front door."

Ken grinned ruefully. "Okay. And I'm sorry about this. I'll be more careful in the future." With that, he left.

Mr. Hardy escorted the boys into his room. A man, who had been sitting in an armchair, got up to greet them.

"This is Will Archer, a secret agent for the Treasury Department," Mr. Hardy introduced him. "He's on the case because it involves money and securities."

"We've had a bank robbery," Archer explained. "The thieves got away with a million dollars and some international securities that were to cover a debt by a foreign government to American banks. It'll be a disaster if we don't get those back before they're smuggled abroad!"

"How did it happen?" Frank asked.

"The gang broke into a sporting-goods store across the street from the bank," Mr. Hardy said. "They came in the middle of the night and got into the basement of the store, where they chipped the plaster off one wall and removed the bricks behind it. They apparently knew that there was a tunnel running across the street to the bank. They went through that passageway and broke through to the bank. There they grabbed the night watchman and tied him up. Then they raided the vault."

Joe's eyebrows shot up. "Can the night watchman identify the burglars?"

Fenton Hardy shook his head. "They were wearing masks. The guard couldn't see their faces."

Frank grimaced. "That's the second time within the past two days that we've been out-foxed by masked men," he said and described the two strangers who had attacked Ollie Fernandez on Lake Algonquin.

"Well, I'm sure there is no connection," Mr. Archer said. "And for the time being, let's stick to this case."

Mr. Hardy agreed. "You're right, Will. This has priority. Let me tell you the rest of the story, boys. The night watchman managed to free himself from the ropes the crooks had used to tie him up. He triggered a manual alarm. When the thieves heard it go off, they came out of the vault with the loot. They ran through the tunnel back to the sporting-goods store just before the police arrived."

"One of them took a diamond ring from a safe-deposit box," Mr. Archer added. "I suppose he would have taken more if the guard hadn't sounded the alarm."

"So the crooks got away with a million bucks, a diamond ring, and the securities," Joe summed up the situation.

"That's it," Mr. Hardy said. "I called you in on this because it's a big case and we have to solve it in a hurry."

"But remember, it's top secret!" Mr. Archer stated. "We don't want—"

Frank interrupted the secret agent by holding up his hand. He had heard a furtive sound outside the window on the fire escape.

"Shh!" he warned.

5 A Mysterious Call

Frank signaled to the others, then went across the bedroom and flattened himself against the wall on one side of the window. Joe did the same on the other side. Mr. Hardy and Will Archer ducked out of sight behind an armchair at the opposite end of the room.

Stealthy footsteps descended the fire escape from the floor above. A pair of battered shoes came into sight, followed by a rough pair of corduroy pants and a leather jacket.

Frank and Joe pulled back before the man could see them. He stopped in front of the room and listened carefully for any sound inside. Then he pushed open the window and climbed over the sill. The boys noticed he had a crooked nose and shifty eyes.

Before he could step forward, they closed in on him. "Care to identify yourself?" Frank asked quietly.

The man spun around, startled, and glanced furiously at the boys. Then he bolted for the door, only to be met by Fenton Hardy and Will Archer, who quickly subdued him.

"Good work, boys," Archer complimented the young detectives. "This is Blinky Haynes. Your father put him behind bars some years ago. But he escaped."

"What made you choose this place to rob, Blinky?" Mr. Hardy asked the intruder.

"I thought it was empty!" the man rasped. "Anyway, you got nothing on me. You can't prove a thing!"

"We don't have to. The old charges are enought to put you away for a long time," Mr. Hardy said as he dialed police headquarters.

Soon a squad car arrived and Blinky Haynes was taken away.

"Do you believe he really just wanted to burglarize the room?" Frank asked his father.

Mr. Hardy shrugged. "He had reason to believe the room was empty. Will and I went out just before you two arrived and we came back through the rear door. If he was watching the front, he didn't see us. And he didn't know you. He had no idea you would come to this room."

"I don't like this," Will Archer said. "Blinky isn't just a casual burglar. I have a feeling he's in with those bank robbers. They must have found out you're on the case, Fenton. Maybe he was sent to plant a bomb!"

"I tend to agree with you," Mr. Hardy replied. "Luckily, we caught him!"

"I'm sure they'll send someone else," Will Archer went on. "You must be extremely careful!"

"I will be, don't worry."

"I have to leave," the agent announced. "Let me know how you and your sons are coming along with this investigation."

"We will," Mr. Hardy promised, and Will Archer, after saying good-bye to everyone, walked out the door.

"What'll we do next?" Frank asked his father.

"I think you should go to the scene of the crime," Mr. Hardy said. "Since my cover may have been blown, I think I'll lie low for a while. I'll move to a different hotel and use a disguise. You two ask Ken Bulow to give you another room under a different name, okay?"

"Fine," Frank said. "Who do we see at the scene of the crime?"

"Mr. Arthur Michaels, the owner of the sports shop. I'll phone him and tell him you're coming. I'll also alert Mr. Barcross, the bank manager." Mr. Hardy made the two calls, then gave the boys directions. "I won't be here when you come back," he said. "I'll contact you as soon as I can."

"Okay, Dad," Frank said. "We'll get going on this right away."

The boys left the hotel and walked a few blocks to a building with a sign over the door reading: THE SPORTS CENTER. The large front windows on either side of the door were filled with displays of sporting equipment. There were tennis rackets, golf clubs, baseball bats, and skin-diving gear. A rubber raft was in the center of one window. Life jackets hung on racks beside it.

"I bet Ollie's using a raft just like that," Frank said.

Joe nodded.

"It's about the right length, and a crew of four could handle it. Boy, I really hope we can run the Roaring River with him!"

"You and me both!" Frank said wistfully.

The young detectives entered the sports shop. Inside, customers were wandering around looking at the equipment. Frank and Joe asked to see Mr. Michaels, and a clerk pointed to a tall, stout man.

When the owner heard who his visitors were, he beckoned them to follow him to his office. After he had closed the door behind them, he said, "I didn't want to talk outside. None of the staff knows about the robbery, because the authorities want to keep the news from getting out." He took off his thick glasses and polished them nervously. "Now, what can I do for you?"

"We would appreciate it if you could tell us the whole story with all the details," Frank said. "And then we'd like to look around for clues."

Michaels fidgeted with his glasses. "I've been through all this with the police," he complained.

"We know," Frank said. "But we only heard a summary of what happened, and we really have to get a firsthand report from you."

"Well, the thieves disconnected the alarm system in our basement," Mr. Michaels began. "I don't know how they did it without setting it off. Then they were able to get in, knock some plaster off the wall, and uncover the tunnel that leads to the bank."

"Did you know the tunnel was there?" Joe asked.

"Of course not, young man!" Michaels replied sharply. "It was already covered up when I bought the building." He pulled a sheaf of documents out of his desk drawer. "Here are all the papers I got from the real-estate company, including a layout of the building. There's no tunnel shown on it, neither is it mentioned in any of the documents."

Frank riffled through the papers. "The previous owner, according to these, is a Mr. Edmund Crowley," he said. "Do you know where we can get in touch with him?"

"You can't," Mr. Michaels replied. "He's dead. The police already checked. And they can't find the people who owned the building before that."

"Somebody on your staff may have found out about the tunnel," Frank pointed out.

The store owner shrugged. "I wouldn't know, but it's possible."

"We'd like to walk around the place," Frank said. "Do you mind?"

"No. Go right ahead. But remember, it's a secret investigation. Pretend you're interested in sports articles."

"We don't have to pretend," Joe said. "We *are*

interested in white-water rafting."

The store owner seemed startled. "You—run the rapids?"

"We have done quite a bit of that and may do some more in Maine," Joe explained.

Mr. Michaels did not comment. Instead, he motioned to the door. "Go ahead and look around," he said. "And let me know if you find out anything."

When they were outside, Frank spoke to his brother in a low tone. "Did you notice that Mr. Michaels seemed upset when he heard we were interested in rafting?"

Joe nodded. "Of course, it could simply mean that he's afraid of rafting because he tried it once and got dumped in the river."

"True," Frank admitted, "but I think we should keep an eye on him."

The boys circulated through the store. They watched the clerks while they inspected the equipment.

"Hello, Frank and Joe Hardy!" A voice suddenly called out.

The greeting took them by surprise. They looked up and saw a girl about their own age, who was obviously in charge of the tennis department.

"How do you know our names?" Joe asked.

The girl smiled. "You two won the tennis doubles match in last year's Eastern High School tournament. I saw you on television. Boy, you really knocked the cover off the ball."

Frank sighed in relief because she apparently did not suspect why they were in the store.

"I'm Marge Stafford," the girl went on. "And I'm really pleased to meet you."

The young people shook hands, then Frank said, "I bet you have more tennis equipment in the basement."

"I wouldn't know," the girl replied. "I just took this job for the summer. And Mr. Michaels declared the basement off limits. I don't know why."

Just then a customer came up to buy a pair of tennis shoes, and the Hardys took the opportunity to move on. After a few moments, Frank nudged his brother. "Don't look now, but we're being shadowed," he whispered.

Joe lifted a golf club and pretended to inspect it while he glanced out of the corner of his eye. He saw a tall, thin man with blond, wavy hair behind them. "I went right by him before," Joe said in a low tone. "The name on his badge is Bill Black."

As the Hardys walked on, Bill Black kept following them. The boys strolled in between two

41

rowboats. Joe, who was in front, kept moving and circled around the left boat, while Frank stayed where he was. He inspected the oars, with the sales clerk close behind him.

A moment later Joe came around, effectively trapping Bill Black between him and his brother.

"May I help you?" the sales clerk asked just when Frank was about to speak to him.

"No, thanks. We're just looking," Frank replied. "Are you in charge of the whole store?"

"Mr. Michaels is. Do you want to see him?"

Frank shook his head. "I was just wondering. You followed us from the tennis department to the golf department and now you're here."

"I thought you might want help," the clerk insisted. "And I can sell items from any department. But if you're not ready yet, please browse further. I'll be here if you need me."

With that, the clerk hastily turned and pushed past Joe. A moment later he was out of sight.

6 *The Dark Tunnel*

"What did you think of Bill Black?" Frank asked his brother.

"I think he acted pretty suspiciously. If he wanted to help us, why did he wait so long, trailing us through the whole store?"

"Let's mention him to Mr. Michaels," Frank said, heading for the owner's office.

Mr. Michaels was surprised when the boys told him about the salesman, but promised to watch Black from now on. "Have you found any other clues?" he asked.

Frank shook his head. "Do you remember anything out of the ordinary the night of the robbery?" he questioned.

"Or just after it," Joe added.

The man stroked his chin with his fingertips. "Well, there was one thing," he said.

"Tell us about it," Frank urged.

"The day after the robbery, a man phoned. He said he saw six life jackets on display in the store. He wanted to buy them."

Frank looked puzzled. "What's so strange about that?"

"I told him he couldn't have them because I had already sold them. He got pretty nasty. I told him we would be getting another shipment soon, but he snarled at me that he wanted the ones he saw. It was quite strange."

"Did he give you his name?" Frank inquired.

"No. As a matter of fact, when I asked him, he hung up."

"I wonder why the man wanted those particular life jackets," Frank said thoughtfully.

"I have no idea," Mr. Michaels said.

"Were they in the store on the night of the robbery?"

"Yes. They were on a display rack near the rowboats." Mr. Michaels ran a hand through his hair. "I wish you boys could come up with an answer to this whole mystery."

Does he really mean it? Frank wondered. Or is he putting on an act? Aloud, he said, "We'd like to have a look at the basement and see how the burglars got into the tunnel."

"I'll take you," Mr. Michaels offered. He led them down a staircase behind his office and snapped on the lights. They saw heavy crates piled on top of one another labeled Skis, Track Shoes, and Football Helmets.

"This is where I keep the inventory," the store owner informed them. "As soon as we sell out an item upstairs, we bring up more from the basement, if we have it in stock. Now, if you go past that pile of boxes over there, you'll see the window where the thieves broke the alarm system."

The Hardys moved around a stack of cartons holding hockey pucks, and walked toward the window. Joe was in the lead. Suddenly Frank saw one of the boxes move. It teetered on the edge of the pile, then fell over and hurtled down toward Joe!

Instinctively Frank grabbed his brother by the arm and pulled him back. The carton landed on the floor with a terrific thump, whirling up dust.

Joe gulped. "That's a pretty heavy box!"

"Golf balls," Frank read the label. "It would have knocked you out if it had hit you!"

Mr. Michaels hurried up to them. He was car-

rying a long pole with a hook on one end.

"I hope you're all right!" he said. "I saw the box from the other side. It was stacked lopsided and I tried to pull it back, but instead it fell. I'm sorry about that!"

He looked flustered and was obviously embarrassed. Frank and Joe were more suspicious of him than ever.

"Here, I'll go first in case there are any more accidents," Michaels offered, and walked to the small window. One pane had been cut. A wire hung on the wall to one side. The cable to which it had been fastened lay on the floor.

"It was a professional job," Frank noted. "The burglars cut the window, then one of them reached in and broke the cable. That shut off the alarm. They must have known exactly where the cable would be. But the window is too small for anyone to crawl through."

Mr. Michaels gestured helplessly with his hands. "They got in through the back door upstairs. Once they disrupted the alarm, they were able to open the door with no one the wiser."

"They probably had skeleton keys," Joe said. "Any gang *that* experienced would have. They just unlocked the door and walked in."

"That's right," Michaels said. "They could have stolen anything in the store!"

"It's interesting that they didn't," Frank said.

Michaels shrugged. "Why would they carry out sports equipment if they can find a million in cash next door?"

"I suppose you're right," Frank admitted.

"Let's take a look at the secret tunnel," Joe suggested.

"This way," Michaels said.

He led them to the back wall of the basement. A mass of broken plaster lay on the floor. Bricks were scattered here and there, and dust covered everything. The dark opening of the tunnel at floor level showed where the plaster and bricks had been knocked from the wall.

Frank got down on his hands and knees. He poked his head into the mouth of the tunnel. Michaels explained how it had been sealed up by the bricks covered with a smooth coating of plaster.

"Amazing," Joe said. "I wonder why it was camouflaged like that." He kicked a brick with his foot, nudging it to one side. A piece of paper came into view, and he stooped down to retrieve it. Glancing at it, the boy realized it was a diagram of some kind. Quickly he thrust it into his pocket before the store owner could see it.

This could be a clue, Joe thought to himself. No sense in letting a suspect see it.

"You boys shouldn't go into the tunnel," Michaels warned. "It could be dangerous. Besides, the police already checked it out."

"We have to see for ourselves how the burglars got into the bank," Joe declared. "Right, Frank?"

"Right."

"Well, suit yourselves. I'm going back to my office," Michaels declared. "I'll see you later." He went up the basement steps as Frank took a deep breath.

"Come on, Joe. Follow me." He moved forward on his hands and knees, using his pencil flashlight to guide him. After a few minutes, the light went out.

"Oh, no!" Frank groaned. "The battery must be dead. Joe, do you have your light?"

Joe felt in his pocket. "It must have fallen out!" he exclaimed. "Now we're stuck in the dark."

"We'll feel our way ahead," Frank decided, putting out a hand before he moved on. At one point the tunnel made a bend to the left.

"Watch out for a left turn," he warned his brother. "I almost dented the wall with my head!"

"Okay," Joe said. The dust made him sneeze. Then he heard the sound of rumbling engines and the squeal of tires above them.

"That's Washington traffic," Frank said. "We must be right in the middle of the street."

Joe was beginning to feel claustrophobic. "I should have brought a can opener in case we get stuck," he tried to joke.

"Just hang in there," Frank said. "It can't be too far to the other end."

The boys pushed on until Frank saw a sliver of light up ahead. "I think we're getting there," he declared. "Just a bit—"

He broke off suddenly as he heard a rattling sound behind him. Turning his head, he saw earth and stones cascading from the ceiling of the tunnel!

While Frank watched in horror, Joe was buried under a mound of debris!

7 The Guard's Story

Frantically, Frank swiveled around on his hands and knees. Burrowing into the debris, he grabbed Joe by the shoulders and dragged him out. Joe was groggy but he soon recovered.

"Are you okay?" Frank asked. "Think you can go on?"

"No problem, Frank, once I catch my breath."

"I wonder why the ceiling collapsed like that. Michaels said the police checked the tunnel. How come they overlooked a weak spot? Say, do you suppose Michaels is responsible? Maybe he followed us and pulled a stone loose with his pole!"

"He might have," Joe admitted. "I wasn't paying much attention to anything behind me, and I didn't hear anything until the roof caved in."

Eager to get through the tunnel, the boys crawled forward as fast as they could. Finally they reached the opening that led into the bank and climbed into a small room where a policeman was on guard.

"Who are you?" he demanded, taken by surprise, his gun at the ready.

"Frank and Joe Hardy," Frank said.

"What are you doing here?"

"Our father told the bank manager we were coming," Frank said. "We're investigating the burglary."

"I'll have to check that," the guard said. He went to a wall phone and dialed a private number, never letting the boys out of his sight.

"Mr. Barcross?" the policeman said. "Two boys just surfaced through the tunnel. They claim they're Frank and Joe Hardy—oh, all right."

"It's okay," the guard said, returning his gun to its holster. "The manager will be right in."

A moment later a middle-aged, dark-haired man walked into the room. "I'm Lawton Barcross," he said, identifying himself. "I didn't expect you to come through the tunnel, but I'm glad you're here."

"May we see the vault?" Frank asked.

"Certainly. By the way, the people down here are the only ones who know about the robbery, and they have been sworn to secrecy by the police. Follow me."

They went out of the room into a corridor lined on one side with heavy metal bars. A large steel door gave access to the interior of the vault. Its lock was burned and twisted.

"That's where the crooks used acetylene torches," Frank inferred.

"But first they short-circuited the alarm system," Joe surmised.

Barcross nodded emphatically. "They ducked under the photoelectric beam. Then they used a magnet to hold back the pin of the alarm mechanism under the mat in front of the door."

"Mr. Barcross, what about the alarm system inside the vault?" Joe queried.

The bank manager grimaced. "That system isn't in place yet. You see, we just took over this building. It's only temporary. We'll be moving into our new building in a few months. I thought everything was secure enough, but I hired a night watchman just to be sure. He's on duty whenever the bank is closed."

Entering the vault, the bank manager showed the young detectives the safe where the money and securities had been locked up. The marks of an acetylene torch were visible on its door. One safe-deposit box was wrenched open.

"That was done with a jimmy," Frank observed, pointing to the box.

"And a diamond ring was taken," Barcross lamented. "I feel terrible that a customer of the bank lost the ring. I hope you boys can get it back for her."

Frank nodded toward the employees who were working in the vault. "It could be an inside job," he said in an undertone. "Maybe one of them is a member of the gang. He could have told them where to find the million bucks and the securities."

Barcross frowned. "I hate to think anyone in the bank would be a criminal. But I can't deny that you could be right."

"It doesn't have to be somebody working in the vault," Joe interjected. "Other people in the bank must have known where the stuff was stored."

Barcross became agitated. "You're right! A number of tellers knew, and so did the officers handling the accounts of the foreign government that owns the securities. FBI agents are discreetly questioning them one by one. But what will you boys do?"

"I think we should talk to the night watchman first," Joe said.

"That's a good idea," Barcross responded. "I guess you consider him a suspect. After all, he knew about the security system and how to short-circuit it. If you want to question him, I have no objection. If we don't retrieve the stolen property, the bank will be ruined—not to mention a scandal!"

Frank nodded. "Where can we find the night watchman?"

"He's at his home," Mr. Barcross replied. "His name is Harry Justo, and he lives on 15 Maple Drive. That's in Georgetown in the northeast section of Washington." The boys said good-bye to Mr. Barcross, left the bank, and caught a taxi for the ride to Georgetown.

They found Harry Justo living by himself in a small apartment. When he answered Joe's knock, he kept the chain on the door and glared at them.

"Who are you?" he growled.

"Frank and Joe Hardy."

"Never heard of you."

"We've been asked by the bank to investigate the robbery," Frank explained, "and we have to talk to you."

"I've already told the police everything I know. Now beat it!"

The night watchman started to close the door but Joe put his foot in the crack. "Mr. Justo," he said, "we're private detectives. If you talk to us, we may spot a clue nobody else noticed."

Frank added, "And if we find the criminals, you won't be under suspicion any longer."

Justo saw the point. He opened the door, let the Hardys in, and motioned them to a couple of chairs. "Sit down," he said and moved toward the sofa. "What do you want to know?"

"What happened on the night of the robbery?" Joe replied.

The watchman stroked his chin. "Well, I made my rounds as usual around midnight. The room the thieves later got into was okay. So, I went past the vault and walked upstairs to check everything there."

"How long were you gone?" Frank asked.

"Well, it takes me about a half hour to circle through the building and get back to where I started. So, the thieves had that much time. They must have hidden in the tunnel till they heard my footsteps die away. Then they cut through into the room."

"When did you find out they were in the bank?"

"When I came down in the elevator. They must have watched the lights because they knew the elevator was descending. As the door opened and I stepped out, they jumped me."

"What did you do?" Frank queried.

"There was nothing I could do. Four of them were on me before I knew they were there."

"Did you recognize any of them?"

"Impossible! They were wearing masks. I couldn't see their faces. They took me to the room where they had dug up into the bank."

"We know they tied you up," Joe informed him. "And we know you got free. How did you do that?"

"The one who did the tying didn't make the knot tight enough. I was able to pull the rope loose. It took me a long time because one of the thieves was watching me. But finally I got one hand loose and hit the manual alarm on the wall."

"That must have caused some action!" said Frank.

"It sure did! The thieves came running out of the vault. One of them carried a briefcase."

"That must have held the money and the securities."

"I guess so."

"And they disappeared into the tunnel?"

"Yes, except that something strange happened."

Joe pricked up his ears. "What was that, Mr. Justo?"

"I thought the whole gang was gone, and I was unwinding the rope around my legs, when one more thief came running out of the vault. I could see he was holding something shiny in his hand. It must have been the diamond ring!"

8   A Warning

"So the last thief was far behind!" Frank said.

Justo nodded. "He jumped into the underground passageway when the police sirens were already sounding and the patrol cars were converging on the bank. But he still escaped. By the time I showed the officers the tunnel, everyone had gone."

The night watchman had no further information, so the Hardys went back to the Grandison Hotel and checked into a different room from the one in which they had met their father earlier that day. When Joe took off his sports jacket, he suddenly remembered the piece of paper he had picked up at the tunnel entrance.

He pulled it out of his pocket and spread it on the table.

"Look what I found," he said to Frank. "I didn't mention it then because Mr. Michaels was with us."

Frank stared intently at the diagram. "It's a sketch of two buildings connected by an underground passage!" he exclaimed.

"Built in 1890," Joe added, noticing the date in the lower right-hand corner. "I bet this is the original plan for The Sports Center and the bank. The tunnel must have been dug when the two buildings were being constructed."

Frank pointed to the words "Library of Congress" stamped at the top. "Somebody found this diagram there," he said, "and realized that an underground passageway led to the bank. With that information, either this person or others associated with him planned the break-in!"

"During which they dropped the plan by mistake, no doubt," Joe finished the thought.

Frank scratched his head. "Here's something else, Joe. What do you make of it?" He pointed to two symbols, $+-$, written in red ink at the bottom of the diagram.

"It's a plus and a minus sign," Joe said. "And it looks as if they were written a short time ago. The ink seems fairly fresh to me."

"Maybe the guy who masterminded the robbery used those symbols to give orders to the gang," Frank surmised.

While they were pondering the mystery, the phone rang. It was Fenton Hardy.

"Did you get another room?" he asked.

"Yes. We're in room 15," Frank replied.

"Good. Be there at six o'clock. I have important information for you. How are you making out?"

Frank explained about the tunnel and mentioned the diagram Joe had found.

"It must be a copy," Mr. Hardy said. "Why don't you go to the Library of Congress and find out who photostated the original document. You have time before our meeting."

"We will," Frank said, then hung up.

The boys walked about ten blocks to the library and asked for directions to the manuscript room, where architectural plans for Washington were kept. A short time later they were looking through a portfolio on buildings in the same block as the bank.

"Here it is," Frank whispered as he lifted a paper out and showed it to Joe. It was the original of the diagram showing the two buildings connected by the tunnel. The plus and minus symbols were missing.

The boys took the sketch to the woman at the

reference desk. "Do you remember someone making a copy of this lately?" Joe inquired.

"Oh, I remember him all right," the young woman replied with a smile. "He had black hair, a black mustache, and a black beard. He also wore dark glasses. I recall thinking that you couldn't tell whether he was good-looking or not because very little of his face was showing."

"Can you tell us his name?" Frank asked. "We'd like to talk to him about this diagram."

She consulted a register. "John Jones," she read the entry.

Looking at the signature, the boys saw a thin, spidery handwriting. "He was left-handed," the librarian informed them.

The young detectives thanked her, returned the portfolio, then left the manuscript room.

"Obviously that man was disguised," Frank said. "And he wrote left-handed to fake his signature."

Joe nodded. Suddenly he grabbed Frank's arm. "Look!"

From a side room, a man wearing thick-lensed glasses emerged and hurried toward the stairs.

"Arthur Michaels!" Frank exclaimed.

"Let's talk to him!" Joe urged.

The boys raced to the staircase and caught up

with the store owner at the bottom.

"Hello, Mr. Michaels," Joe said casually. "Have you read any good books lately?"

"I was reading about white-water rafting," Michaels replied. He seemed nervous.

"Have you ever seen an old architectural plan for The Sports Center?" Frank inquired.

"Only the one I received from the real-estate agent when I bought the building," Michaels replied. "I told you that. Now, I have to be going. I hope you'll solve your case." With that, the man turned on his heels and left.

"Maybe he came to the manuscript room in disguise," Joe muttered.

"It's possible," Frank said. "But what really gets me is that white-water angle. A raft seems to be floating into our bank-robbery investigation all the time!"

The boys returned to the Grandison Hotel. Shortly before six there was a knock on their door. Expecting their father, Joe opened the door and a man pushed past him into the room. He had black hair, a black mustache, and a black beard. His eyes were hidden behind tinted glasses!

Frank leaped up from the easy chair he had been sitting in. "Joe! Lock the door!" he hissed.

Joe turned the key and pocketed it. The man

looked surprised. "You got nothing on me!" he said in a squeaky voice. "You can't hold me here!"

"You came in here, remember?" Joe said. "And you're not leaving until you give us an explanation about what you were doing at the Library of Congress!"

"I wasn't at the Library of Congress!" the man said, suddenly in a familiar voice.

Frank and Joe burst out laughing. "Dad!" Frank exclaimed. "It's you!"

"I'm glad my disguise works," Mr. Hardy said, taking off the glasses. "If you didn't recognize me, no one else will, either! Now, what was that about the library?"

"Someone that looked just like you in that disguise made a copy of the original building plan for the bank," Frank explained. "It contained the tunnel."

Mr. Hardy chuckled. "This is the first time I unwittingly chose the same disguise as a suspect. He could be the man I came to talk to you about. His name is Wolf Erskin. He and a number of other men are wanted for several bank robberies committed in different states. An undercover agent spotted Erskin in Washington the other day, but then lost him. I don't know where he is now."

"My guess is there's a connection between the bank robbery, The Sports Center, and white-water rafting," Joe said and told his father about the meeting with Mr. Michaels.

Mr. Hardy nodded thoughtfully. "You may be right. Especially since someone wanted those life vests from the sports shop and Ollie Fernandez has been losing his up in Maine. I've got things under control at this end now. Why don't you go to the Roaring River and check out the Fernandez expedition."

"That's fine with us," Frank said.

"Just one word of warning. If there is, indeed, a connection and Wolf Erskin is involved in this case, watch out!" Mr. Hardy pulled a photo out of his pocket. "That's Erskin. Memorize his features. This man is as dangerous as a rattlesnake!"

9 *Undercover Crew*

Frank and Joe flew back to Bayport the following morning. They picked up their yellow sports sedan at the airport parking lot and drove home.

Mrs. Hardy and Aunt Gertrude were in the living room. "Where's your father?" Mrs. Hardy asked.

"Oh, Dad had to stay in Washington," Frank explained. "We haven't solved the bank case yet, but he knows the prime suspect, so he felt he didn't need us any more."

"Good. The grass needs cutting," Aunt Gertrude declared.

"I'm afraid we won't be around for long," Joe

said. "We're going up to Maine to follow up on a clue."

"In Maine?" Aunt Gertrude's eyebrows shot up.

"We have a hunch that Ollie Fernandez's expedition on the Roaring River has something to do with Dad's case," Joe said and told his mother and aunt what they had found out in Washington. "We're going to call Jack Wayne and see if he can fly us up tomorrow."

"This way we can crew for Ollie at the race, too," Frank added with a smile.

"I don't know if I like that!" Aunt Gertrude declared. "Suppose the raft sinks?"

"Oh, don't worry, Aunty," Joe said and put an arm around his relative. "How can it sink, with us on board?"

Frank had already gone to the phone and was talking to their friend Jack Wayne, who was a private pilot. Jack often flew Mr. Hardy on his missions and knew the boys well.

"It's good to hear from you, Frank," the pilot said. "My schedule is clear for tomorrow, so we can start early. Be at the airport at seven, okay?"

"Great!" Frank exclaimed. "See you then." He hung up, then dialed police headquarters. A moment later, he was connected with Chief Collig.

"Any news on that stolen car used by the two masked men at Lake Algonquin?" he asked.

"It was returned to the owner, Frank. We found no clue in it. And there's no trace of the men who took it."

Frank was disappointed. After saying goodbye to the chief, he put in a call to Chet Morton. "We're flying to the Roaring River tomorrow morning," he said. "We'll pick you up at six-thirty."

"That's the middle of the night!" groaned Chet, who preferred to snooze in bed instead of getting up early.

"You don't have to come," Frank needled him. "Sweet dreams!"

"Oh, I'll be ready!" Chet exclaimed. "Don't you dare leave me behind," he added anxiously.

Frank chuckled. "We wouldn't leave without you, Chet. We need your muscle on the raft!"

The Hardys left the house at six in the morning. Joe drove their car to the Morton farm, where Chet climbed in with them. Then they went directly to the airfield, parked, and entered the main building. They found Jack Wayne in his office. He was examining maps of Maine.

"What part of the Allagash Wilderness

Waterway do you want?" he queried.

"The Roaring River," said Joe. "It's at the far northern end, near the Canadian border."

Wayne picked out a large-scale map of the area. "Here it is," he commented. "The airstrip is marked. It won't be hard to find. Come on."

They took off in Jack's small plane, *Skyhappy Sal*, with Chet sitting beside the pilot. Frank and Joe were in the back seat. They circled over Bayport and flew north until they saw the Maine woods below their wings.

Suddenly Chet heard a ticking sound under his seat. He turned pale.

"It's a bomb!" he cried out. Before Jack had a chance to comment, Chet reached down and pulled a package from beneath the seat. Then he wrenched the door open and threw the package out.

In his eagerness he lost his balance. With a scream, he plunged forward and out the plane!

Acting by reflex action, Frank lunged across the back of the seat and thrust out an arm. His fingers closed around Chet's belt. Desperately he held on until Joe grabbed Chet's shoulders. Together they drew their friend back.

"Chet, you almost jumped into the Maine woods!" Frank gasped. "Without a chute!"

Chet was pale and shaken by his close call.

He asked to change places with Joe to get away from the door. Then he managed to mumble, "Anyway, I ditched the bomb!"

Jack Wayne shook his head, his face still tense after the near disaster. "That was no bomb, Chet. That was a clock. I was taking it to my grandmother in Bangor on the return flight to Bayport."

"What!" Chet's face became red with embarrassment. "It—it—oh, I'm so sorry!"

Joe leaned out to pull the door shut. Then he started to laugh. "Jack, you can still take the clock to your grandmother!" he announced. "The string is caught on the plane's undercarriage. Frank, if you'll hold on to me, I'll get it back."

"Sure," Frank said and anchored his brother around the legs. "Go ahead."

Joe placed one hand against the fuselage, reached down with the other one, and drew the package into the plane. Then he closed the door.

Not long afterward, they landed at the Roaring River airstrip. Jack Wayne helped the boys lift their bags out of the cockpit.

"Are you sure you'll be okay?" he asked. "You won't be able to hitch a ride around here. This place is pretty desolate."

71

"Ollie gave us directions," Frank said. "We'll be fine."

"Well, I'm off then," Jack said and climbed into the cockpit again.

The three boys followed the trail Ollie had described. A short walk brought them to the river, and after a while they spotted the cabin on its bank.

Ollie saw them and came outside. "I spotted the plane coming in for a landing," he said with a big grin. "I was hoping it would be you."

He showed them into the cabin, which was made of split logs. "You can sleep over there," Ollie said, pointing to three bunks along one wall in the bedroom. A helmet and life jacket lay on each bunk.

The boys stowed their gear, then Chet grabbed his helmet and plunked it on his head.

"Okay, I'm ready," he announced with a grin.

"Chet, the problem is to find a life jacket big enough for you," Joe quipped. "You'll never get into a regular size."

Chet looked offended. "They're adjustable, aren't they?" he asked.

"Don't worry," Ollie said. "We'll find one that fits you. Now come on out and meet the others."

Ollie's crew was working behind the cabin

on the equipment. He introduced Frank, Joe, and Chet as the new members of his expedition. "As I mentioned before, these fellows will ride the raft with me," he said.

A tawny-haired youth named Tarn was sanding an oar. He gave the newcomers a friendly smile and shook hands with them. "I'm sure glad to see you," he said. "I'm a whiz with the boats. But I've never run the rapids, and I sure don't want to start now."

"We're depending on you to keep the gear in shape, Tarn," Frank smiled. "Without you, we're not going anywhere."

Chet pulled *Running the River Rapids* out of his pocket and showed it to Tarn. "I've been studying up on the subject for weeks," he said. "And the Hardys have lots of experience. Together we can't lose!"

Tarn took the book and opened it curiously. "Ah, here's some good advice," he said with a grin. "What to do if you fall into the water!"

Chet shrugged. "It won't happen."

Tarn gave him an ironic look. "You haven't seen the rapids yet."

Frank and Joe, meanwhile, were talking to the other three members of the crew. Two of them, Bruno and George, were friendly. The third, a husky boy named Karl, smiled coldly.

"Actually, we don't need anybody else on the expedition," he said. "We could have handled it just fine ourselves. But now that you're here, I suppose you might as well help." He turned and walked over to the river.

"I wonder what's eating him," Joe whispered to his brother. "He acts as if we're about to let the air out of his raft."

"He obviously wanted to be on it," Frank said. "He resents the fact that Ollie brought in more people."

"Or maybe he doesn't want us around for other reasons," Joe pointed out. "He could be in with whomever was stealing those life jackets."

"It's possible."

Chet and Ollie joined the Hardys at that moment. "How about a walk in the woods?" their host suggested.

Frank and Joe realized that he wanted to talk to them confidentially, away from the others.

"Sure," Frank agreed. "We should familiarize ourselves with the surrounding area."

Ollie led the way through the trees until they were beyond earshot of the camp, then stopped under the outspread branches of a tall pine.

"I haven't told anyone that you're detectives," he revealed. "I wanted you to investigate without anyone suspecting you. Have you noticed anything strange yet?"

"Karl isn't very friendly," Joe said. "He made it quite clear that he doesn't want us around. He could be involved with the thieves who stole your life jackets."

"Karl?" Ollie was shocked. "I can't believe that. I think he's just jealous. He wanted to run the rapids with me, you know. But he has no experience, so I'm glad you could make it."

"Well, you may be right," Frank said. "But since he was the only one who was really disturbed about our coming here, we have to watch him."

Ollie nodded. "I understand. Now tell me, how did you make out in Washington?"

"We can't talk about the case," Frank replied. "It's to be kept secret. But let me ask you something, Ollie. Where did you buy those life jackets that were stolen?"

"From a place called The Sports Center in Washington," Ollie replied.

10 Rivals!

Frank and Joe looked at each other. They had suspected this for quite a while.

"Did you buy *all* your life jackets from The Sports Center?" Frank inquired.

"No. Only the six new ones. I have others from previous expeditions that we're still using."

"Is there anything special about the new ones?" Frank asked.

"They're lighter and stronger than the old models," Ollie replied. "I saw them advertised in a Sports Center catalog, and I ordered half a dozen."

"If you bought six, and only five were stolen,

that leaves one jacket from The Sports Center," Frank summed up the situation.

"Yes. The one I was wearing on the lake when I was attacked," Ollie said. "It really looks as if those guys weren't after my life, but the vest I was wearing. But why? What do they want with those six jackets? They can buy them for a lot less trouble than it took to steal them."

"I'm fresh out of ideas," Frank admitted.

"Do they have any special markings?" Joe asked. "Anything that will help us identify them?"

"Each has The Sports Center logo, two red circles, one inside the other," Ollie replied.

"Someone had to tip off those masked men that you were taking your life jacket with you when you went home," Frank stated. "Nobody knew that except the members of your crew, right?"

Ollie looked troubled. "I suppose not."

"I'm sorry, but it seems as if somebody here is your enemy," Frank said. "It could be Karl!"

"If he's guilty, I want to prove it," Ollie said. "We don't have much time left before the race. And tomorrow another shipment of life jackets is due from The Sports Center." He paused a moment, then went on, "The only people I can think of who would want to sabotage the race are our competition. I think you have to check out Brian Schmidt's people."

"We will," Frank replied. "Where is their camp?"

"About a mile downsteam from us, on the other side of the river. You can take one of our canoes. Tarn'll give you one. He's in charge of the boats."

The boys went back to the cabin, where Ollie asked Tarn to lend the Hardys a canoe.

"Give me twenty minutes," Tarn said, "and I'll have one ready to go."

Actually, he had one available in less time than that. "This one is in good shape," he declared when he took the boys to the spot in the river where the craft were moored. "You can paddle it down the whole Allagash Wilderness Waterway if you want to."

Frank laughed. "We don't need to go that far. Not today."

Chet decided to remain at the camp and keep an eye on Karl, so Frank and Joe set off together. The swift current caught them and swept them out into the middle of the river. Suddenly a large wave hit them broadside, threatening to capsize the canoe. Joe expertly held his paddle in the water, allowing the following wave to strike the flat part of the blade, while Frank, in the stern, paddled strongly on the other side. The bow turned downstream and they took advantage of the current to move on swiftly.

"This river's tricky, all right," Joe said.

"It sure is," Frank agreed. "Hey, look, I see a cabin down there. Must be Schmidt's place. Let's pull over."

Frank and Joe trailed their paddles and guided their boat in a wide arc toward the bank. As the bow headed into the shallow water, Joe jumped ashore and tied the canoe to a tree. Frank followed him and they looked around.

They saw equipment for running the rapids, including a rubber raft the size of Ollie's that was drawn up on the bank. Four oars were lined up in the bottom of it, with four white helmets next to them. Four life jackets were draped over the side.

Joe quickly checked them out. "No red circles on these," he declared. "They aren't the ones stolen from Ollie."

"His might be somewhere else," his brother replied. "Keep an eye peeled and maybe we'll find them."

The crew of the rival expedition was working in front of the team's cabin. One of the members now came toward the Hardys. He was whittling a tree branch with a long, sharp hunter's knife and gave them a threatening look.

"Hi," Frank said.

"Hello," the young man replied guardedly. "I'm Brian Schmidt. Who are you?"

"We just joined the Fernandez crew," Frank said. "I'm Frank; this is my brother, Joe."

By now the rest of the Schmidt expedition had crowded around the newcomers, giving them hostile stares.

"What are you doing down here?" Schmidt demanded. "Are you spying on us?"

His query caused angry exclamations from his friends.

"Let's throw them in the river!" one man called out.

Schmidt held up a hand. "We can do that later, Ormsby," he said. "First, we find out why they came."

"When we get involved in a sports contest, we like to meet the competition," Joe said. "Nothing wrong with that, is there?"

"In other words, you *are* spying on us," another crew member declared.

Schmidt waved the sharp point of his knife at the Hardys. "Well?" he rasped.

"Besides wanting to meet you," Frank said evenly, "we'd like to ask you if you have seen

five life jackets, by any chance. They were stol-
en from the Fernandez expedition."

"Oh, now they're accusing us of theft!"
Ormsby cried out.

"You have a lot of nerve!" Schmidt agreed.
"Coming here telling us we're thieves!"

"We didn't say that!" Frank protested. "We
were just wondering if—"

"If what?" Ormsby demanded. "The life
vests just walked over here by themselves waiting for you to pick them up?"

A chorus of loud, scathing laughter broke out
among the crew.

"Maybe now Fernandez will have to with-
draw from the race," one of them jeered.
"Wouldn't that be a shame!"

While they had been talking, Brian Schmidt
had quietly walked away in the direction of the
river. Now he came back and pointed his knife
at the Hardys.

"Look!" he declared. "We didn't steal your
dumb life jackets, and we don't want you around.
Now head back for your canoe and get out of
here—and stay out!"

Frank shrugged. "Sorry you feel this way," he
said. Then he turned and pulled Joe by the arm.
"Come on, Joe."

The boys walked toward the river. "They're

following us!" Frank whispered to his brother. "Don't slow down or they may get nasty."

The Schmidt crew tailed the young detectives all the way to their canoe. Frank and Joe got in quickly and started paddling away from the camp.

"I guess it wasn't such a good idea talking about the life jackets," Joe said.

Frank shrugged. "They weren't exactly welcoming us even before we mentioned that. Too bad we didn't have a chance to look around a bit more. The only life vests we saw were not from The Sports Center."

"I wonder what makes those jackets so valuable to whoever stole them," Joe said. "And I wonder if Mr. Michaels knows."

"Or Bill Black, the store clerk who followed us," Frank added.

"We don't know for sure if he was following us," Joe said. "Maybe he was just doing his job."

Frank nodded. "We don't know for sure whether Schmidt took the life jackets, either. Maybe he just didn't want anybody to butt into his operation. When we mentioned the jackets, he got mad because he realized we suspect him."

"So many maybes," Joe said, "It's aggravating."

The boys were so preoccupied with the mystery that they had stopped paddling without noticing it. The canoe started to drift downstream.

Suddenly Frank snapped to attention. "Joe, we'd better paddle or we'll wind up in the rapids!"

The Hardys wielded their blades vigorously. The canoe began to move upstream, and with long, steady strokes Frank and Joe picked up speed despite the strong current. They passed trees, bushes, and boulders in the shallow water and soon came within sight of their cabin.

Suddenly Joe felt water splashing around his feet. He looked down and saw a trickle seeping in through a crack in the hull.

"Frank, get ready to bale!" he said over his shoulder. "We're shipping water!"

"Keep paddling, Joe. Let's see if we can make it to the bank."

Frank had scarcely spoken when the cracked birchbark gave way, and the force of the current drove a stream of water into the canoe. A moment later, their boat began to sink!

11 A Friendly Offer

As the canoe sank under them, Frank and Joe scrambled into the river. Turning the boat over, they swam to the bank pushing it ahead of them. Frank climbed out of the river and grasped the bow while Joe pushed at the stern. They maneuvered the canoe onto shore and paused to catch their breath.

Joe wiped the water out of his eyes. "Whew!" he gasped. "What made it sink like that? Tarn said we could paddle it all the way down the waterway!"

"He was wrong," Frank said, and walked around the canoe to inspect it. Suddenly he stopped short. "Look at this!" he cried out and pointed to the break in the bow where the water had come in.

Joe joined him and saw that a square patch of birchbark had given way under the force of the current.

"The canoe was sabotaged!" Frank exclaimed. "Somebody cut halfway through the birchbark and left the river to do the rest! He knew the patch would give way and we'd sink!"

"Whoever it was got at the canoe while we weren't around," Joe pointed out. "Say, Frank, it could have been Brian Schmidt! You remember how he left us while we were talking to his crew. He went down to the river and saw our canoe. At that point he could have cut the birchbark. He had enough time. With that hunter's knife of his he could carve a whole canoe into kindling in nothing flat!"

"Unless someone did it earlier at our cabin," Frank said. "Tarn could have done it, or whoever it is who works against Ollie."

"True," Joe admitted. "Another maybe. It's driving me crazy."

The boys walked to the cabin, where they found Ollie and the others preparing to go for a practice run. Frank and Joe explained what happened to the canoe.

"That's pretty low of Brian Schmidt," Ollie said angrily.

"If it was Brian," Joe pointed out. "We're not sure."

"It must have been," Tarn insisted. "I checked the canoe and I didn't see any cut-out patch."

Joe shrugged. "It may not have been that visible," he said.

"It makes me feel terrible!" Tarn said. "Maybe you guys think I did it!"

"No, we don't," Frank said. "Don't worry about it."

Tarn seemed upset. "I do worry about it. But it won't do any good. Anyway, I'll go fix it." With that, he left. Ollie and the others followed him outside, but Frank and Joe stayed behind to change into dry clothes.

First they showered. When they had finished and were about to walk into the bedroom, a movement caught Frank's eye. He pulled Joe aside and gave him a signal. Both boys flattened themselves against the wall on opposite sides of the doorway and peered cautiously into the room.

Karl was moving silently along the bunks until he came to Ollie's. The life jacket marked by the two red circles of The Sports Center in Washington was hanging on the wall next to the bunk. Karl reached up and removed it from its hook.

"He must be the thief!" Joe whispered hoarsely.

Frank nodded grimly. "Let's get him before he takes off with Ollie's Jacket!"

The Hardys stepped forward. Hearing their footsteps, Karl whirled around and stared at them.

"I thought you *had* a life jacket, Karl," Frank said.

"I did, but it was stolen," Karl said sullenly. "So I decided to borrow Ollie's."

At that moment, Ollie walked in. "I'll need it myself," he told Karl. "I want to go out and practice with the Hardys and Chet."

Karl shrugged. "Okay. I'll take one of the old ones." With that, he stalked out of the cabin.

"Do you think he was telling the truth?" Joe asked his brother.

"He's still a suspect," Frank replied. "He may be the one who's in cahoots with Brian Schmidt's group to sabotage the Fernandez team."

Ollie looked doubtful. "We do borrow each other's gear sometimes, you know," he said.

"I know," Frank said. "We just have to look at every angle."

The boys spent the rest of the day practicing on the river in canoes. When they came back, Ollie conducted a strategy workshop.

"Let's review some of the basics," he said. "Chet, what do you do when you fall off the raft?"

"Float on my back downstream with the current," Chet replied.

"And go feet first," Joe added, "so you don't bump your head on a rock."

"Right," Ollie said. "Now, what's the best way to guide a raft through the rapids?"

"All four men have to handle their assignments properly," Frank replied. "The lookout in the bow spots the rocks and shouts directions for getting around them. The sweep in the stern uses his oar to steer. The two oarsmen in the middle provide the muscle to keep the raft going."

"What if the rapids are too narrow?"

"The two in the middle ship their oars," Joe answered. "They pull them into the raft and let the current carry it along. Otherwise they're liable to break an oar on a boulder—which means the race is over for that crew."

Suddenly the boys heard a small plane approaching over the treetops. It came into sight as the pilot circled for a landing.

"That must be the plane with the new shipment of life jackets!" Ollie exclaimed. "It will also have supplies for us. Let's go over to the airstrip."

The boys started to run along the trail toward the landing field, but after a few steps Frank grabbed his brother's arm.

"I'd better stay," he said. "If no one's in the cabin, the thief might sneak back for Ollie's life jacket."

"Good idea," Joe said and ran on.

Frank returned to the cabin and sat down on his bunk. He found a sports magazine on a table and began turning the pages. Suddenly he heard footsteps outside.

He jumped up and hid behind the door. A moment later, the door was pushed open and Karl stepped into the bedroom. Frank stood stock still and the boy did not notice him. Instead, he went to Ollie's bunk and looked at the life jacket again. He reached out to take it off the hook, then changed his mind, and went into the bathroom.

A moment later, Joe walked noiselessly into the cabin. Frank motioned to his brother to join him at his hiding place.

"Karl left the others," Joe whispered. "I followed him here. I don't know what he's up to."

"He came in, and now he's in the bathroom," Frank said.

They stopped talking as Karl emerged from the bathroom. He was carrying something in his hand. The Hardys watched breathlessly to see what he would do next. Again he walked toward Ollie's bunk. Frank's body tensed, ready to go into action. But Karl passed the bunk and sat down on his own. He opened his hand and the young detectives saw that he had been holding a bottle of iodine. Now he raised the left leg of his jeans and applied the iodine to a cut above his knee.

Just then a gust of wind blew the door shut with a loud bang. Startled, Karl looked up. He saw the Hardys.

"What is it with you guys?" he demanded. "You seem to like the game of hide and seek!"

"We stayed behind to see if someone would come to steal Ollie's life jacket," Frank explained. "It's the last one of that shipment that hasn't been taken yet."

"I bet you thought I'd take it," Karl said, his eyes full of hostility. "You suspect me because I looked at it. I was only wondering what was so special about it. As if that was a crime!"

"Look, Karl, nobody's accusing you of anything," Frank said. "I only explained why we stayed behind. Ollie asked us to keep our eyes open because he had five life jackets stolen, all from the same shipment, and one is left. It stands to reason that someone might be wanting that one, too. No one said you were that person."

Karl scowled. "Do what you want. It doesn't mean a thing to me." He dropped his pants leg, got up, and took the bottle of iodine back into the bathroom.

Frank and Joe heard a motor revving up in the direction of the airstrip. "The pilot must be taking off," Frank surmised. Through the window, they saw the small plane zoom up over the treetops, then it disappeared into a mass of white clouds. A few minutes later, Ollie and the others returned to the cabin.

"We got all the stuff we ordered," he announced happily, as he put down a carton of life jackets. The others brought in cases of food and first-aid supplies. When everything was stowed away, the crew prepared dinner, and soon the young people went to bed.

A strange sound awakened Frank in the middle of the night. He raised his head. It was too dark to see, but he realized that the noise came from between his bunk and Ollie's.

He swung his legs to the floor and felt his way forward. As his eyes became accustomed to the dim light that the half-moon cast through the window, he saw Ollie's life jacket move!

Frank reached forward and his fingers touched a furry object. It wriggled free from his grasp, leaped to the floor, scampered to the open window, and a second later, vanished over the sill.

Frank chuckled to himself. A squirrel, he thought. Lucky nobody woke up. I'd have a hard time explaining why I thought a squirrel was running off with Ollie's life vest. He crawled back into his bunk and went to sleep.

In the morning just after breakfast, a man dressed in the uniform of an Allagash Wilderness Waterway Ranger walked into the camp. He was a pleasant fellow with a rugged, outdoors look, and greeted everyone affably.

"I'm Earl Majors," he announced. "I'm going to umpire the race down the river. Who's in charge?"

"I am," Ollie replied, and introduced himself and his crew. "All of us are registered," he added, "except the three new people, Frank and Joe Hardy and Chet Morton."

"Well, I'll register them here and now,"

Majors said and took out his pad. He wrote down their names and told them they were now officially allowed to use the waterway and all its streams for boating.

"Have you been to the rapids yet?" he asked the Bayporters.

"No," Frank replied. "Ollie was going to take us there this morning."

"I'm on my way down there now. Want to come?"

"Sure," Frank said, and the others nodded in agreement.

"Good," Ollie said. "This way I have time to practice."

The four set out on foot with the river on one side and the forest on the other. After a couple of miles, they heard a roaring sound ahead of them around a bend in the river.

"What's that?" Chet queried. "It sounds like a cage full of lions!"

"It's the current hitting the boulders," Majors explained. "That's where the river gets its name. "You'll need to spend some time here and memorize the terrain so you'll know what you're up against when you come down in your raft."

The sound grew louder as the group advanced. Rounding the bend, they saw the untamed river beating its way through a channel it had carved on its way to its meeting with the Allagash River. The water rose in waves, dashed against the rocks, and churned into a white froth.

"That looks worse than any white water we've ever run!" Frank said. "These boulders are big enough to sink a battleship!"

Chet had turned white. "We're supposed to go down—there?"

Earl Majors shrugged. "It was your idea to join Ollie, wasn't it?"

"Maybe I'll change my mind," Chet said.

"I'm sure Karl would be happy to replace you," Joe needled his friend.

Chet shot him a sidelong glance and said no more. As the foursome walked along the rapids, the Hardys memorized the turns and twists of the river as it rushed onward between the boulders. Finally they came to the end of the white water.

"I have to patrol the river downstream from here," Earl Majors announced. "And there's no need for you boys to go with me. When you're finished studying the river, you can follow this trail into the woods and I'll catch up with you later. There's a blueberry patch at the end of the path, and from there it's a shortcut to the Fernandez cabin."

"A shortcut?" Joe asked.

"Yes. It leads across a bend in the river. But you'll have to cross a stream up ahead. You'll find a rowboat tied to a tree. The rangers keep it there in case somebody gets lost in the woods. After you cross, tie it to a tree on the other side. Then follow the trail till you reach the blueberry patch. I'll catch up with you there, say, in an hour or so. That'll give you another half hour to study the rapids."

"Okay," Frank said, and the ranger strode along the river.

The boys spent the time they had surveying the narrow channel of foamy water and finally moved off along the trail through the woods. Suddenly Chet spotted a sinuous movement in the underbrush.

"Look out!" he cried, "there's a rattlesnake in there!"

12 Danger in the Woods

Startled, the Hardys whirled around. Joe noticed a long, thick vine extending through the grass. It rustled slightly as the wind blew its end against a log lying on the ground.

"Look again," Joe told his friend with a chuckle. "Besides, I don't think there are rattlesnakes in Maine. No poisonous snakes live this far north."

Chet gulped. "Sorry, fellows," he apologized. "But it sure looked like a rattler to me."

Soon the boys came to the bank of a wide stream.

"I don't see any rowboat," Frank declared.

"It's not on the other side, either," Joe confirmed after scanning the opposite shore.

"What'll we do now?" Chet asked.

"Well, we have a clear view downstream," Frank reasoned, "so we know the boat isn't there. "Let's walk upstream for a bit. We may find it there."

The young detectives tramped through the forest for about a mile. Then they heard the sound of water plunging down onto rocks. Minutes later they came in view of a waterfall about forty feet high.

Frank was disappointed. "There's no use going on," he stated. "Nobody in his right mind would try to cross that stream in a rowboat above those falls."

"We may be able to cross here," Joe suggested as he approached the waterfall. "There's a ledge behind the falls that looks wide enough."

He stepped onto the ledge. Finding it too narrow to walk on, he balanced himself with his back against the rocky wall. The toes of his hiking boots extended over the edge as he slowly made his way across.

Chet came next and Frank brought up the rear. The cascading water blocked their view, and the thunder from the rocky whirlpool was deafening. They struggled to keep their footing on the ledge as they inched along slowly.

In the middle, the ledge bent sharply to the

right. Gingerly, Joe shifted his feet and turned around, gripping the wall with his fingertips. He edged around the bend, then turned again to face the water.

Chet tried to follow his maneuver. But his fingertips slipped off one of the rocks, and he lost his balance, teetering backward! The plunging water struck him in the face and he almost fell into the rocky whirlpool!

However, Joe reached out in time and grabbed his friend by the left arm. Frank caught his other arm. Desperately the Hardys struggled to hold their footing as they dragged Chet back onto the ledge.

At last they succeeded and paused for breath. "That was a close call!" Frank puffed.

"Too close," Chet gasped. "But I'm okay. I just got my face washed, that's all."

Moving carefully, the three continued their perilous march until they reached the end of the waterfall. Then they walked downriver and got back to the trail that wound through the trees and brought them into a rocky, boulder-strewn area.

A steep hill was on one side and a sheer cliff on the other. Suddenly, a massive boulder crashed down the hill, barely missing Joe! Another fell near Frank.

Looking up, the boys saw a furtive figure flit-

ting among the trees on top of the hill. He picked up another boulder and hurled it at them. Chet ducked just in time. The big rock hurtled over his head and down the cliff, followed by smaller stones mixed with earth.

"It's a landslide!" Chet blurted. "We'll be buried alive!"

"Make a run for it!" Frank shouted from the rear.

"It's too late," Joe called over his shoulder, as a mass of stones and earth cut off his path. "But I see a cave over there. Come on!"

Joe ducked into the cave with Chet and Frank close behind. They turned and watched the debris rain down outside, sending up clouds of dust. In a few moments, the landslide had covered the mouth of the cave, and the boys found themselves in total darkness.

Frantically, they attacked the mound of debris, coughing and sneezing, and tossed stones over their shoulders into the cave. But soon Frank gave up.

"It's no use," he said. "We're trying to dig through a mountain with our bare hands!"

"We're trapped!" Chet lamented. "What'll we do?"

"Earl Majors will come looking for us when we don't show," Joe said.

"Trouble is, he doesn't know we're in this

cave," Frank pointed out. "He—" Suddenly the boy stopped, holding out his hand. "You know something," he said excitedly. "I feel a current of air. Let's find out where it's coming from."

They groped around in the blackness. Joe and Chet felt along opposite walls, while Frank stepped to the rear, holding his hands out in front of him. Suddenly the back wall gave way to empty space.

"I found a tunnel!" Frank cried out. "That's where the air is coming from. Maybe we can get out that way."

The young detectives crawled into the tunnel, and moments later Frank caught a glimmer of light ahead of them. He saw an opening big enough for them to squeeze through.

With cries of joy, the trapped boys made their way out of the cave. Tall bushes sheltered them as they peered cautiously up the hill. The furtive figure was nowhere in sight.

"I suppose he thought he got us for good," Joe said. "Unless he's waiting to ambush us somewhere else. We'd better be careful."

The Hardys and Chet circled the hill, however, without suffering another attack from their unknown enemy. They resumed their trek along the trail, and Chet was the first to spot the blueberry patch. With a big grin on his face, he hurried ahead of his companions and grabbed berries with both hands.

"This is great!" he cried out as he popped them into his mouth.

"I wouldn't mind having some myself," Frank declared and both he and his brother joined Chet in the feast.

Ten minutes later, Earl Majors arrived. "Everything is okay downriver," he announced. "And I see you got here without trouble."

"Not quite," Joe corrected him. "We were almost finished off by a waterfall and by a mystery man!" Quickly the boys filled Majors in on what happened.

"I have no report about anyone out here except the two expeditions!" the ranger exclaimed. "Can you identify this man?"

"No," Joe replied. "He was too far up the hill."

"He may have taken the rowboat," Majors said thoughtfully. "But why would he want to harm you?"

Joe shrugged. "We have no idea." He did not want to reveal anything about their case at this point.

"I'll alert the other rangers on patrol in the forest," Majors promised, "and we'll all look for this guy. But first I'd better take you back to Ollie's camp."

When they arrived at the cabin, the boys invited Majors to have a cold drink, but he declined, saying he had to continue his patrol. The Hardys and Chet went inside and found Ollie sitting at the table with a can of soda.

"Ah, just what we wanted," Chet said and got three more out of the refrigerator. The long walk and their harrowing experience had made them tired and thirsty.

"What do you think of the rapids?" Ollie asked.

"They aren't as dangerous as something else around here," Frank replied.

"What do you mean?"

Frank told Ollie what had happened. "Someone's definitely after us," he concluded.

"Obviously the same people who are after me!" Ollie cried. "What are we going to do?"

"The best thing right now is to scout around the woods and look for clues," Joe suggested. "But one of us should stay behind and watch Karl."

"I'll stay," Chet offered quickly.

"Come down to the river with me," Ollie told him. "I have a practice run scheduled in a few minutes, and everyone will be there, including Karl."

Ollie and Chet went to the water where the raft was already launched. Karl and George joined them aboard, and they pushed into the placid upper stretch of the Roaring River.

Meanwhile, Frank and Joe were circling through the woods behind the cabin. Joe spotted a trail and flattened grass. "Somebody's been through here, heading east," he observed.

"Let's follow the trail and see where it goes," Frank said. "But be careful. Whoever is out there may try to attack us again."

Using their backwoods training, the boys followed the flattened grass until they came to a hiking trail. They scouted the grass on either side without finding any sign of footsteps.

"Whoever came here stayed on the trail," Joe commented, as they moved deeper into the forest. After a while, the trek became more difficult because the trees grew closer together and the underbrush was thicker. The Hardys covered about a mile through tall pines. Their steps made no sound on the thick carpet of needles, and the eerie silence was broken only by the occasional call of a bird.

A sudden sound in the underbrush made them freeze in their tracks. Crouching down, they watched the grass move as the sound came toward them. A bush shook, and a large red fox trotted out. It moved across the trail and disappeared on the other side.

Frank and Joe relaxed. They got up and continued their trek until the trail came to an end. There they saw more bent grass, broken branches, and snapped twigs.

"Looks like a crowd went this way," Joe said.

"According to Earl Majors, no one is around but the expeditions," Frank muttered. "I think we're on to something!"

Joe had hardly finished speaking when the earth gave way under his feet and he plummeted out of sight!

Frank rushed to where his brother had disappeared and looked down. Joe was lying on his back at the bottom of a deep hole. He blinked his eyes, then scrambled to his feet and looked up.

"Are you all right?" Frank asked anxiously.

"I think so. Just get me out of here!"

Frank lifted a long branch from the underbrush and lowered it into the hole. Joe got a firm grasp on the end, wedged his feet against the side of the hole, and pulled himself up step by step. Finally he climbed out and brushed the dirt from his clothes.

"See how damp the earth still is?" he said. "This hole was dug recently. Then it was covered with pine branches to hide it."

Frank nodded. "Whoever dug it wanted to catch the first thing that came along. Probably a deer."

"Well, it sure caught me!" Joe said ruefully.

The Hardys proceeded more cautiously until

they reached a thicket of spreading bushes. Frank pointed to a thread hanging from a thorn. "That came from a whipcord jacket," he said. "We—"

Just then a noise beyond the bushes made the boys freeze. A second later, the foliage parted and two bear cubs appeared, tumbling over and over with each other on the ground. Then one broke loose and ran away, pursued by the other.

The Hardys grinned at the sight. "Too bad we don't have time to watch them," Joe said.

The bushes rustled again, and the next instant the Hardys saw a large black bear following the cubs, its eyes gleaming like coals and its jaws snapping savagely!

The huge animal stopped and looked around. Spotting the boys, it reared up on its hind legs and snarled ferociously. Then it came down on all fours and barreled toward them in a headlong charge! It was too late for Frank and Joe to run away.

Desperately, Frank grabbed a branch of the spreading pine under which they stood and swung up into the tree. Joe reached out, too, and his fingers were clutching the branch when his feet slipped on the needles. He lost his balance and fell down right in the path of the charging bear!

13 Robbers' Roost

As the bear reached for him with its claws, Joe rolled desperately to one side. The ferocious beast hurtled past him into the underbrush, and Joe swung up into the tree beside Frank.

Whirling around, the bear reared up and reached for the boys. It took a swipe at Frank that just missed him. He and Joe climbed up higher and looked down from a safe perch. Gradually the bear stopped clawing at the tree and ceased growling. It got down on all fours and lumbered off into the woods followed by the cubs. The sound of their breaking through the underbrush died away.

The Hardys climbed onto the lower branches

of the tree and jumped to the ground.

"Earl Majors said a black bear can be ornery!" Joe gulped. "Now I know what he meant!"

"You and me both, Joe! Lucky for us that bear went in the opposite direction. I hope we don't meet another one in the woods!"

They moved on following the signs of bent grass and broken twigs. Beyond a row of trees they came to an open, level space that had been hacked out of the forest.

"That's an airstrip!" Joe exclaimed. "You can see the ruts where tires hit the ground!"

"They look like chopper marks," Frank said. "Somebody's been flying in and out."

The Hardys advanced cautiously, watching for danger at every step. Suddenly Frank grabbed Joe by the elbow and pointed ahead. The sound of voices could be heard faintly in the distance.

The boys crept stealthily through the trees. The sound grew louder. They hit the ground and crawled behind a spreading bush. Parting the branches, they peered through.

A small cabin stood in a forest glade, and two tents were pitched next to it. Several men were sitting on the ground in front of the tents. Five life jackets were lying side by side on the grass.

The Hardys recognized the leader of the

group from the picture their father had shown them.

"Wolf Erskin!" Joe gasped. "These are the bank robbers, Frank!"

"And that's Bill Black behind Erskin!" Frank whispered. "The clerk who followed us in The Sports Center! He's one of the gang. He must have shown them how to break into the store!"

"And he's probably responsible for my 'accident' in the tunnel," Joe guessed.

Erksin turned to the man next to him. The Hardys strained to hear what the gang leader said.

"Lewis, I'm tired of waiting for Fernandez to disband his expedition and get out. I wish the director would give us the green light to run him off the river. We could wind up this whole operation!"

"Our guy on the crew said he'd let us know when the time is right," Lewis declared. "He also promised to get the life jacket for us, just like he did the other five. But he has to wait for the right moment. He doesn't want Fernandez to suspect him."

Frank and Joe stared at one another. They were thinking the same thing. Lewis was referring to one of Ollie's crew. Could Karl be the traitor?

"Too bad we didn't get that life vest when we

jumped Fernandez on Lake Algonquin," Erskin complained. "It was such a good plan."

"I got the jacket off him," Lewis grumbled. "But then those Hardy boys butted in. I recognized them from a picture in the newspaper. They once testified against some friends of mine they caught."

Erskin sighed. "It's rotten luck they got involved. This whole thing hasn't been going too well. First you lost that building plan of the tunnel, then Blinky got caught, and the next thing you know, the Hardy boys are snooping around."

"They may even have found that diagram," Lewis replied, "but it won't do them any good."

"It has the symbol on it," Erskin pointed out.

"So what? They'll never figure out what it means. Just like they'll never know what I did with the diamond ring," Lewis snarled.

"You'd better be right," Erskin grumbled. "The director won't like it if you goofed!"

Bill Black stood up. "I'm going to check our trap," he announced. "Maybe a deer fell into it. Then we can have venison for dinner!"

Frank and Joe flattened themselves on the ground and remained motionless with pounding hearts as Black walked past the bush that concealed them. He disappeared into the woods.

They rose into a crouching position and listened again to the men in the glade. But the conversation told them nothing new. Aware that Black was behind them, they were ready when they heard him returning. They ducked under the thicket and lay still until he was past.

"Something fell into the trap," Black informed the rest of the gang. "But it must have jumped out. The hole's empty."

Erskin looked disgusted. "We shouldn't have wasted our time digging it."

A sound in the forest on the other side of the tents made him jump to his feet. "Somebody's coming!" he hissed.

The others leaped up beside him as the footsteps came closer. A shadowy figure emerged from the trees, walked out of the forest and into the glade.

As he advanced toward the cabin, Frank recognized him. "It's the ranger—Earl Majors!" he whispered. "What's he doing here? He told us he was patrolling the river!"

"Maybe he's come to arrest the gang. But he doesn't stand a chance against all these guys. We'd better pitch in and help him, Frank!"

"Not yet," Frank warned. "Something funny's going on. Let's wait and see."

Majors walked up to the men who did not seem surprised to see him. "I have orders from the director," he informed them." But first I want to warn you that Frank and Joe are here!"

The criminals looked stunned. Erskin and Lewis stared at each other, then turned toward Majors. "How do you know that?" Erskin rasped.

"I registered them with the Fernandez expedition. They're the detectives from Bayport all right. I saw their pictures in a law-enforcement journal before I was expelled from the rangers."

"Well, they may be *at* the Roaring River now," Erskin snarled. "But soon they'll be *in* it!"

"Yeah, swimming with the trout!" Lewis added. "They won't get away from us!"

"Forget the Hardys for now," Majors advised them. "We won't be here much longer. I've got our orders from the director."

The phony ranger took a note out of his shirt pocket and held it up for all to see. Each gang member craned his neck for a look at the writing on the paper.

"You know what the symbols mean," Majors continued. "The reason for this order is that the securities from the bank have to be taken abroad as soon as possible. The director has a buyer who wants them in a hurry. That's why we can't wait for the Fernandez expedition to leave the Roaring River. We're going into action soon and we'll pull off the job once and for all."

Majors put the paper back in his shirt pocket. "So how have you been doing out here?" he changed the subject.

"It's tough camping in the woods," Erskin responded. "I'm glad we don't have to stay here much longer."

"The chow is lousy," Lewis grumbled. "Nothing but dry rations all the time."

"Well, you'll only have one more night of it," Majors declared. "Tough it out. When the deal's finished, you'll have more money than you'll know what to do with."

Erskin chortled. "That's what I like to hear!"

"So do I!" cried the others in unison. Then they all laughed loudly.

The crooks discussed dividing the loot as night fell. They lighted lanterns and continued talking, but without revealing anything that Frank and Joe did not know already. However, the boys patiently stayed in hiding, their ears straining to pick up every word.

Finally Majors said, "We might as well go to sleep. We'll strike camp in the morning and move out in the afternoon."

Two of the men went into the cabin, and the others crawled into the tents. Earl Majors stretched out in front of the tents under a spreading pine tree. Soon his regular breathing told the Hardys that he was sound asleep.

The whole camp was quiet. The only sound in the darkness was the screech of an owl winging its way across the underbrush in search of prey.

Frank tugged Joe by the sleeve and gestured to the rear. They moved silently back into the woods until they were out of earshot of the camp.

"Now I know who rolled those boulders off the cliff and almost killed us!" Frank said angrily. "And to think we trusted Majors!"

Joe nodded. "We have to do something!" he said tensely. "Now that we've found the gang, we can't let them escape!"

"We can't do it ourselves," Frank decided. "We have to alert the rangers and have them send out a platoon to round up these people."

"Trouble is, we can't prove anything," Joe pointed out. "They'll deny they ever said what we heard them say!"

"Maybe not," Frank said, his brow furrowed as he thought of a solution to their problem. "If we sneak into their camp, and get the piece of paper Majors showed the others, we'll know what they're up to and can catch them in the act!"

114

"You're going to pull it out of his shirt pocket?" Joe asked incredulously.

"It's the only way. You stay back a little, and if things go wrong and they catch me, you alert the rangers, okay?"

Joe nodded, even though he was uneasy about their daring plan, and the two made their way back to the camp. Frank cautiously inched up to the sleeping man and slowly removed the director's orders from his shirt pocket. He held it up to the moonlight and read it. It said:

COMPLETE OUR PLAN AND ATTACK FERNANDEZ EXPEDITION.

THE DIRECTOR + −

14 Surprise Attack

Frank slipped the paper back into the shirt pocket of Earl Majors. Then he turned and crawled to the edge of the camp where Joe was waiting.

Just before he got there, he heard a voice from one of the tents. "Stop!" Erskin shouted. "I saw you! You won't get away with it!"

Frank and Joe froze for a moment. They started at the tent, but nothing moved. Erskin did not appear, and a moment later, a loud snore followed his outburst.

"He's having a nightmare!" Frank whispered. "Let's get out of here."

"Wait!" Joe said. "How about taking a look at those life vests before we go?"

Frank grinned. "Excellent idea. You want to go this time?"

"Sure." Joe sneaked up to the spot where the five life jackets were still lying in the grass. When he got there, he took out the new pencil flashlight he had brought from home and shone it over the vests. Sure enough, the logo of The Sports Center in Washington—the two red circles—was stamped on each of them.

Joe snapped off his flashlight and quietly made his way back to his brother. Then the two hurried into the woods.

"Those are the life vests that were stolen from Ollie all right," Joe said on the way to their cabin.

"I still can't figure out what the crooks want with them," Frank declared.

"Well, they're obviously after Ollie," Joe reminded him. "They're going to attack his expedition!"

"But they could have sabotaged it much more effectively if they had stolen everything, not just the life jackets!"

Joe shrugged. "True."

With the help of the compass Frank was carrying, the boys tried to find their way through the woods. The moon shone occasionally, but after a while it was covered by a mass of billowing clouds, and the Hardys had to resort to their flashlights.

They struggled through the underbrush, unable to see their way. They stumbled over creepers and felt thorns tearing at their clothing. Small animals scurried out of their way and scared them with sudden noises.

After a couple of hours, Frank came to a halt.

"We should have reached Ollie's camp by now," he said. "Even though the compass indicates we are going in the right direction, I think we're lost!"

"I've been afraid of that for a while," Joe admitted. Then he cocked his head. "Listen, Frank! Over there!"

In the silence of the dark forest, they could barely make out the sound of running water.

"It's a stream, I bet," Joe said. "Must be a tributary to the Roaring River. We can follow it and then walk upriver."

"Good idea," Frank said. "Let's go."

The young detectives found a shallow brook meandering over a bed of pebbles. A short walk downstream brought them to the Roaring River.

Frank pointed to a giant pine tree silhouetted against the night sky. "I remember seeing that tree on our hike down along the river," he declared. "That means the expedition is upstream from here."

The Hardys set out at a rapid pace. They reached the camp as the sun was rising. Ollie Fernandez was alone on the river bank inspecting the raft.

"I'm glad to see you guys," he said as he greeted them.

Frank and Joe collapsed, exhausted. "We had a long walk in the woods," Frank said. "And we found the gang of crooks that stole your life jackets!"

"What!" Ollie stared at them with a mixture of surprise and admiration.

"You have a traitor among your crew," Joe went on." We don't know who he is, though. And these men out there in the woods are planning to attack your cabin!"

"But—but who are they and what do they want?"

"We only know three of them. One is a man sought in the case we were working on in Washington," Frank said. "A second works at The Sports Center there, the other is Earl Majors."

"The ranger?"

"Ex-ranger," Joe corrected Ollie and told him what they had overheard.

Ollie ran a hand through his black hair and sighed. "Boy, were we duped. What are we going to do now?"

"Alert the Waterway Rangers," Joe replied. "The real ones. Do you have a walkie-talkie in the cabin?"

"Yes. You can do the talking," Ollie said. "You're more experienced with that type of thing."

They went into the cabin and Ollie handed the walkie-talkie to Joe, who got in touch with ranger headquarters. Quickly he identified himself and explained to the officer on duty that Wolf Erskin and his notorious gang of bank robbers were camped out in the woods near the Roaring River. "They pulled off that bank heist in Washington," Joe added.

"Wolf Erskin, eh?" said the officer. "I wouldn't believe it from anybody else. But the word of the Hardy boys is good enough for me. Our choppers will leave immediately. One will touch down at your airstrip."

Frank outlined a strategy while they waited. "We don't want to question the others in your expedition yet, Ollie. We suspect Karl, but we don't have any proof. So we'd only put him on guard. We'll play it cool and see if he tips his hand."

"Okay, I'll go along with that," Ollie declared. "I just hope it doesn't prevent us from getting ready for the race."

"It won't," Joe promised. "We won't say a

thing to anyone except Chet till we have the evidence. The expedition can go on as usual."

Half an hour later, a ranger helicopter landed at the airstrip near the Fernandez expedition. The officer took Frank and Joe aboard.

"We're going in first," said the pilot, who identified himself as Captain Lecore. "Three more choppers will land directly on the airstrip in the woods Joe mentioned."

Lecore covered in minutes the distance that had taken the Hardys hours on foot. He met up with the other three choppers in the air, and they flew in a random pattern so as not to arouse the suspicion of the crooks. When they came close to the criminals' campsite, they zoomed in and landed quickly before the gang had a chance to disperse.

In minutes, the rangers had the camp surrounded. Erskin and Lewis broke through the line and ran into the woods.

Erskin dodged between the tall pines. Frank ran after him and began to catch up. The criminal swerved to the left, but Frank headed him off and brought him down with a flying tackle. They rolled over and over on the ground. Frank came out on top and pinned Erskin down until a ranger came up and slipped a pair of handcuffs on the crook.

At the same time, Joe was in pursuit of Lewis,

who ran frantically until he tripped over a vine and fell into the underbrush. Joe pounced on him and applied a wrestler's hammerlock. Another ranger rushed to the spot and hand-cuffed Lewis.

The two crooks were escorted back to the rest of the gang. They glared furiously at the Hardys.

"We've met before," Joe said. "But this time we get to see your faces instead of your masks!"

"What do you mean?" Erskin snarled.

"You were trying to steal Ollie's life jacket on Lake Algonquin, remember?"

Lewis shook his fist. "We should've knocked you off!"

Frank shrugged. "You weren't enough of a wrestler for that."

"Come on," the rangers said, "over to the chopper." They led the men to the helicopters while Frank and Joe stepped up to Earl Majors, who was staring at the ground with a guilty look.

Frank drew the paper out of Majors's shirt pocket and handed it to Lecore.

The ranger read the message. "Who's the director?" he demanded.

Majors refused to answer. Lecore asked Erskin. "I don't know," the gang leader confessed. "Majors and Black were the go-betweens. I never met the director."

"What do these plus-minus symbols mean?"

"They're the director's code. But I don't know what they stand for. Majors knows."

Joe confronted Majors, but he refused to talk. "Well, we'll find out eventually," the boy said. "Just as we found out you've been working with the gang all along. You set us up when you showed us the trail to follow, and shadowed us after your phony excuse that you had to patrol downriver. That rowboat you told us about was a myth! But you knew about the cave and hoped to trap us in there after you rolled the boulders down on us."

"I still can't figure out how you got out of there," Majors scowled.

"You should have scouted it better, and you might have found the tunnel we used!"

Frank turned to Erskin. "Where are the securities and the million dollars stolen from the bank?"

"You should know if you're so smart," the gang leader snarled.

Joe challenged Lewis. "What did you do with the diamond ring from the bank?"

Lewis smirked. "That's my secret, and I'm not telling you. You wouldn't find it in a million years!"

15 To Catch a Thief

Much as they tried, the Hardys could not get anything out of Lewis or any other member of the gang, and finally gave up the interrogation.

"They're hardened criminals who won't talk," Lecore said. "But they won't rob banks any more when they're behind bars, either. You boys were a big help!"

"We always work with the law-enforcement agencies, if possible," Frank said. "I suppose that's why we trusted Earl Majors when he told us he was a ranger."

"He used to be one," Lecore said, "until he was expelled from the organization for illegal activities. Since then, we have had reports about his impersonating a ranger. We've been searching for him. Now, thanks to you boys, we've got him."

"One other thing," Frank said. "Those five life jackets over there—the ones marked with red circles—belong to Fernandez. They were stolen."

"We'll see that the expedition gets them back as soon as I make my report," Lecore promised. "Too bad we didn't find any of the loot from the Washington bank robbery."

The helicopters took off for the Waterway Ranger Headquarters. One of them touched down to let the Hardys out at the airstrip near Ollie's cabin.

"I'll be back to umpire your race with the Schmidt expedition," Lecore said. Then, with propellers whirling, his chopper lifted away from the forest.

Frank and Joe walked down the trail to their camp. The crew was standing outside the cabin.

"We saw that chopper come in," Karl said suspiciously. "What was that all about?"

Joe waved his hand airily. "We hitched a ride back from the woods because we were lost. Luckily the rangers found us."

Karl looked at him as if he did not believe him, then turned and began polishing his crash helmet.

Ollie changed the subject. "We had a great

practice today," he declared enthusiastically.

"Especially me!" Chet boasted. "I sure moved the raft with my oar! No problem!"

Ollie cautioned him, "That's only upstream where there are no rapids. It'll be different when we go through the white water, Chet."

The reminder of the foamy, turbulent channel put a damper on Chet's good mood. "I suppose so," he said lamely.

Everyone went inside for a snack and talked about the next practice run, while Frank and Joe took a nap. Some time later, they woke up and signaled Ollie to follow them outside. Chet came along, too.

"Have you two thought about who the traitor could be?" Frank asked Ollie and Chet.

"No," Ollie said sadly. "I watched everyone closely, but didn't notice anything suspicious."

"What about Karl?" Joe asked.

"I watched him," Chet said. "But he didn't do anything. Besides, I talked with him a few times. He's not the friendliest guy around, but once you get to know him he opens up a little. I really don't think he's the one, Joe."

The sound of the cabin door opening caused them to turn around. Karl came out and strolled toward them. "If you guys can go for a walk in the woods," he stated, "I guess I can too." He went into the bushes on the river bank. They heard his footsteps die out among the pine trees.

An idea struck Joe. "Ollie, nobody else in the expedition knows the crooks have been caught, do they?"

"No. We saw the ranger helicopter land, and we saw the other choppers in the sky. But that doesn't mean anything. Ranger aircraft fly over the forest all the time on patrol duty. There's no reason why the thief in the expedition should suspect anything."

"All right, then. Let's set a trap for him," Joe continued. "He thinks he's still working for the crooks. He thinks they want that sixth life jacket—yours, Ollie. Suppose you leave it where the thief can get at it. We'll be there and catch him when he tries to steal it."

Frank took up Joe's idea. "Ollie, leave your life jacket outside the cabin tonight. We'll set up an ambush."

"Okay, you've convinced me," Ollie agreed. "What do we do till nightfall?"

"Joe and I will go over to Brian Schmidt," Frank decided. "It's clear now he didn't steal the life jackets, and I have a feeling he didn't cut our canoe, either. Anyway, if we go and apologize for suspecting him, maybe he'll be a little friendlier and we'll pick up a clue."

"Go ahead," Ollie said. "You can use that canoe over there."

The boys paddled diagonally down and across the river and went ashore near their rival's cabin. Brian Schmidt and his people saw them coming and waited in silence as the boys walked up to them.

"Hi," Schmidt called out finally. "What brings you guys back here?"

"We came to tell you that we caught the people who stole our life jackets," Frank said.

"You mean we're vindicated?"

"Well, we did suspect everyone in the area," Joe admitted. "Wouldn't you have?"

"I suppose so," Schmidt replied. "And since it's time for confessions, we have to tell you something, too."

He motioned to an upturned boat. "Sit down."

Frank and Joe took seats, then Schmidt continued. "I know we were rather rude to you when you came here before. The reason was that we were warned by someone that you were spies who would try to sabotage our expedition."

"What!" Joe exclaimed. "Who said that?"

"A man named Earl Majors," Schmidt replied. "He said he was a ranger and told us that two guys were around, hired by Ollie Fernandez, to get us into trouble."

"Earl Majors is a crook!" Frank cried out.

"We found out that he was dismissed from the rangers and is up to no good. Captain Lecore dropped by and told us," Brian Schmidt replied. "We talked about going over to Ollie's place and talking to you, but we decided you probably wouldn't even let us put ashore after the way we treated you."

"I'm glad it's all cleared up," Joe spoke up and started to shake hands with the members of Brian's expedition. "You really had us wondering what your game was, and we weren't looking forward to the race against a hostile team. But we can't blame you for acting as you did under the circumstances."

"Thanks," Ormsby said. "Thanks for not holding it against us."

Joe chuckled. "You'd have been even angrier if you'd known what else we suspected you of. You see, someone cut out a piece of our canoe and we almost drowned on the way home last time. Since Brian had gone down to the river carrying his knife that day we were here, we thought he'd done it."

Brian stared at him. "I went to look at your

boat because I was afraid you might have brought something to—well—to sabotage our camp!"

Joe nodded. "I understand. Meanwhile, we found out that there's a traitor in our *own* expedition, and we're sure he was responsible."

"Do you know who he is?" Ormsby inquired.

"No. That's the problem. We hope he'll give himself away before the race," Frank replied.

"I hope so, too," Brian said sympathetically.

The young people discussed the race for a while, then Frank and Joe paddled back to the Fernandez camp. Nobody was there, so they circled the cabin, looking for a place to set a trap for the traitor. They found a solitary pine tree behind the building. It had a low-hanging branch on which Ollie's life jacket could be fastened. A nearby maze of bushes and creepers would provide a good hiding place for the boys.

They had just returned to the cabin when the crew came back from the river. While the others were taking their showers, the Hardys told Ollie about their talk with Brian Schmidt and the tree outside the cabin where the ambush would be set for the thief.

"You and Chet can join us while we keep watch," Frank said.

"What excuse will I give for the four of us being away tonight?" Ollie asked.

"Tell them we're going over to spy on the Schmidt expedition. Since you've suspected them all along of trying to sabotage you, it makes sense that we'd try to find out what we can."

Ollie grinned. "Great idea!"

When supper was almost over, he casually announced, "I'll be away from camp with Frank and Joe and Chet tonight—until morning. You guys stay on the alert while I'm gone."

"Where are you going?" Tarn inquired, his eyebrows raised.

"We want to spy on Schmidt and his crew," Ollie said. "We know that they're out to get us, but we can't prove it unless we find out what they're up to. We're hoping to pick up a clue."

Karl looked concerned. "Maybe you should take some more men with you," he suggested. "That way you can split up and cover the entire camp."

"I thought of that," Ollie replied. "But the more of us there are, the more we risk being discovered."

Karl shrugged, but said nothing, and the four left the cabin. Ollie carried his life jacket with him and hung it over the branch of the pine tree. He made sure it was clearly visible from the back windows, then he walked with his companions toward the river, where they got into a canoe and headed downstream. Once safely around a bend and out of sight from the camp, the boys pulled quietly to shore and beached their canoe under cover. Then they ducked into the thick woods, made a wide circle on foot, and cut back toward the cabin from the rear.

Frank and Joe took up positions on opposite sides of a growth of pine saplings, while Chet hid behind a bush. Ollie dropped down and lay prone in the underbrush. In the moonlight, they all could see Ollie's life jacket hanging from the branch of the tree.

They waited until the last light in the cabin went out.

"I hope the trap works," Ollie whispered.

"I do, too," Frank muttered, "but we may have to wait a while longer."

The time stretched into a half hour, then into another half. Chet fidgeted. "What if nobody comes?" he worried.

"Then we're out of luck," Joe told him, "but we have to take the chance."

The minutes ticked away as the night wore on. Chet tried hard to keep his eyes open, but finally his head began to nod and suddenly he emitted a loud snore.

Joe crept over and shook him by the shoulder.

"Stop making noises!" he said in a low tone. "Your snoring would scare anybody away within a mile!"

"I wasn't snoring!" Chet said defensively, "just resting."

"Well, rest quietly!" Joe hissed. He crawled back to his position and ducked down, afraid even to swat at a mosquito buzzing around his ear.

Beams of moonlight filtered through the trees and illuminated the bait. Joe could even make out the two-circle logo from The Sports Center in Washington.

Then clouds drifted across the moon and cut off the light momentarily. A second later, a figure materialized from the darkness at the corner of the cabin. Quietly he moved through the underbrush toward the pine tree. When he arrived, he reached out and took the life jacket from the branch and turned to go.

Chet rushed forward and clutched him in a bear hug, as Frank snapped on his pencil flashlight and directed the beam toward the intruder's face. They all stared.

"Tarn!" Ollie gasped.

16 Ollie's Hidden Treasure

Tarn turned pale as Ollie snatched the life jacket from his hand.

"Obviously *you're* the one who took all the life vests!" Ollie said accusingly. "Why did you do it?"

Tarn was shaking with fright. Realizing that he had been caught red-handed, he leaned limply against the tree.

"A gang of crooks made me do it," he confessed. "I ran into them one day when I was hiking in the woods. They threatened me, and I had to go along."

"Threatened you with what?" Ollie demanded.

"Well, you see, I—" Tarn choked for a moment, unable to go on. When he had collected himself, he spoke in a flat, subdued voice. "It's a long story. I got into trouble with the law when I was fifteen. A few buddies and I stole a car to sell for parts and make some money. My father had left my family when I was two. My mother was sick, there were six other kids, and most of the time we were hungry."

He sighed and went on. "I know that's no excuse, but anyway, I wound up in a juvenile detention center. It was a terrible place. I could tell you stories that'd turn your stomach. After a year, I managed to get out of there—escape, I mean. I met a writer who did a lot of white-water rafting. He took me on as crew and taught me how to take care of the equipment. However, a few months ago he went to Europe.

"I found out about this expedition, and because I was good at maintaining equipment, you hired me. I told you I was eighteen, but I'm really only sixteen. If the authorities find out about me they'll ship me back to the detention home."

Tarn paused a moment, his voice breaking. "Everything went just fine for a while, until I ran into those guys. One of them was Matt Lewis. I don't know how he found out about me, but he knew. He told me all he wanted was the six life jackets from that place in Washington. If I didn't deliver, he'd make sure I'd get turned over to the cops. I told him I couldn't steal them all at once. If I walked out with the whole bunch of them at one time and I got caught, how would I explain it? He said to take whatever I could grab."

"Did you tell this Matt Lewis that Ollie had taken his jacket along when he went home?" Frank inquired.

"I had to. By that time Ollie's was the only one left. When Ollie left with it, I thought I was in trouble. What if he didn't bring it back? Anyway, Lewis told me to get it the day Ollie left."

"It almost cost Ollie his life," Joe pointed out. "Lewis and a man named Erskin ambushed him on Lake Algonquin and almost drowned him, trying to steal his vest."

Tarn looked shocked. "I had no idea—"

Joe did not let him finish. "Why did you slash a hole in our canoe when we went to see Brian Schmidt?"

"When Lewis found out that you and your brother had joined the expedition, he told me to get rid of you. I figured if I sank the canoe, you would make it to shore, but maybe you'd get scared and go home."

Tarn ran a hand through his hair and sighed.

"Believe me, a couple of times I was tempted to tell you the whole thing, Ollie, and be done with it. But then I thought of going back to that horrible place, and—and I just didn't have the nerve to do it. I suppose now you're going to turn me over to the cops," he concluded in a hushed voice.

Ollie looked at the boy for a long moment. "You've been a good worker," he said. "I'm willing to give you another chance." He glanced at the Hardys. "What do you think?"

"I think that's very decent of you," Joe replied.

"But when the gang finds out I told you, they'll get me anyway," Tarn said.

"No, they won't," Frank whispered. "They've been arrested by the rangers and are in jail!"

Tarn's eyes showed his surprise. "They are? Wow! I don't believe it! Ollie, I promise—I'll never let you down again. I'll work hard and—"

"Okay, kid," Ollie said with a grin. "And we won't tell the others anything, don't worry."

The boys sent Tarn back to the cabin, then crept back through the woods to return by canoe after sunrise, as if they had spent the night at Schmidt's camp. Ollie explained that they had found no clues, and after breakfast he announced that the expedition would have another practice run on the river and study the rapids.

"There are only two days left before the race," Ollie continued. "We've got to see that everybody here is really up to it."

They donned their life jackets and crash helmets. Frank, Joe, Chet, and Ollie were just filing out of the cabin when the walkie-talkie sounded. Ollie went back to answer it, and the Hardys and Chet waited for him.

"This is Captain Lecore," said the voice on the other end. "Are you people ready for the race the day after tomorrow?"

"We sure are," Ollie replied.

"Good. I'll umpire, as I told you before, and one of my men will fire the starting gun. When the race is over, I'll present the prize to the winning team."

"We'll be looking forward to receiving it," Ollie said with a grin.

Captain Lecore chuckled. "Good luck to both you and Brian Schmidt."

Ollie snapped off the walkie-talkie, and turned to go. Suddenly Joe had an inspiration. "I just thought of something," he said. "Ollie, take off your life vest for a moment. I'd like to inspect it."

"You have the same type," Ollie pointed out. "It came in the second shipment from The Sports Center."

"But yours is the one Lewis wanted," Joe said.

Ollie shrugged and took off his life jacket. Joe turned it over and looked at the tear Ollie had sewn up with the leather cord. He ran his thumb along the seam and then felt just below the tear.

"There's something underneath that cut," he said. "Do you mind if I cut the cord?"

"Go ahead," Ollie said, looking puzzled.

Suddenly Frank saw the light. "Joe! You think that maybe—"

Joe nodded. "Give me your knife, will you?" Frank handed Joe his pocketknife and Joe pushed the tip of the blade under the lowest strand of the leather cord. With a single twist of his wrist, he sliced the cord through all the way to the top. The tear fell open. He placed his thumb at the bottom of the hole and pushed upward. A small object emerged and fell out. Joe caught it with his other hand and held it up. It sparkled in a ray of sunlight slanting through a cabin window.

"The diamond ring we've been looking for!" Frank cried out.

Ollie was flabbergasted. "Has that ring been in my jacket all the time?"

"Ever since you bought the jacket!"

"I never noticed when I sewed the tear. But how did the diamond ring get into the vest?"

Joe explained. "After Lewis and his buddies robbed the bank in Washington, he was the last one to leave. The police had already begun to converge on the scene. He had the ring and obviously didn't want to get caught with it. So, when he ran through the sports shop, he saw the life vests on display. He quickly cut into one, hid the ring, and figured he'd retrieve it later, provided he didn't get caught."

"I get it," Ollie said. "If the police arrested him empty-handed, he might have gotten away with a lesser sentence."

Frank saw where Joe's logic was leading. "Lewis thought he could get the ring back by buying the life jacket. He returned to the store, but found all six of them gone. So he called the manager, Mr. Michaels, under the pretext he wanted to buy all six, to find out what happened."

"And when he heard they had been sold, he was plenty mad," Joe finished. "Through Bill Black, his contact in the store, however, he discovered that the life vests had been sold to you,

141

Ollie. Since he wanted the ring, he knew the only way to get it back would be to find that life jacket. But he didn't know which vest the ring was in, so he told Tarn to steal them all."

Ollie scratched his head. "Why didn't he just ask Tarn to get the jacket with the tear?"

"He was afraid Tarn would examine the tear, find the diamond, and run off with it."

"I get it," Ollie said. "When the first five jackets revealed no tear, Lewis knew *my* jacket contained the ring. So he followed me home and ambushed me on the lake."

Suddenly Frank spotted a shadow moving outside the cabin. He gestured to the others to be silent, and pointed to the window. They turned and saw a face peering over the windowsill at them. It was a man with black hair, a black mustache, and a black beard. He wore spectacles tinted so darkly they could not see his eyes.

"It's the guy from the Library of Congress!" Frank shouted. "The one who copied the architect's diagram!"

The man pulled back from the window, then they heard the sound of feet running into the woods.

"We've got to catch him!" Joe exclaimed.

The boys dashed out the door and around to

where the mysterious prowler had been. The noise he made in the underbrush was becoming fainter. They ran in that direction. Chet tripped over a creeper and fell into a thicket. Frank stopped to see if his friend was all right.

"I've got some scratches," Chet grumbled, "but we'll never catch up with that guy now."

"Joe will," said Frank confidently. "Come on! We may still get a piece of the action!"

They ran on again and caught up with Ollie. "Joe's way ahead of us," Ollie reported.

Although hampered by the life jacket he was wearing, Joe closed the gap between himself and the fugitive. The sounds in the underbrush became louder. Joe spotted the man through a grove of trees.

Quickly the young detective moved through the dense vegetation. A large thorn caught in his life jacket and held him back. But he wrenched himself free and continued the pursuit into an open glade in the forest.

A small unmarked plane stood in the clearing. The man ahead of him was racing toward it. Joe cut in at an angle in an effort to head him off. The man swerved away and got to the plane with Joe only steps behind.

As he jumped through the open door into the cockpit, Joe made a flying leap and grabbed him by the leg. The man tried to kick himself free while Joe struggled to pull him out of the cockpit. The battle raged. Joe was successfully dragging his antagonist out of the plane when the man suddenly reached down to the ground and grabbed a handful of dirt. He hurled it at Joe, who felt it sting his eyes. Blinded momentarily, the boy lost his grip.

He heard the door of the cockpit slam shut, and the motor start. He rolled free of the craft and wiped his eyes clear of grit just in time to see the plane race down the strip and take off. A moment later it disappeared over the treetops.

Joe was looking disconsolately after the plane when his three companions came up.

"He got away," Joe lamented. "Just when I thought I had him, he threw dirt in my eyes."

"Did you get a good look at him?" Frank asked.

"I got a good look at his disguise, since I was close enough to count his whiskers. But I wouldn't know him from Adam if I ever saw him without his beard and sunglasses."

"You two seem to know something about this guy," Ollie surmised as they walked back from the glade.

"We haven't met him before, but we heard about him," Frank said, and described their visit to the Library of Congress, where they had found that a man answering the stranger's description had copied the architect's diagram.

"He's the one who learned about the underground tunnel leading from The Sports Center to the bank," Frank concluded.

Ollie scratched his head. "But how did he fly in here without our hearing him?"

"Since he didn't come that close to our camp, we probably paid no attention," Frank said. "The rangers fly over the area all the time."

"And he obviously knew about the glade," Joe noted, "because the gang spotted it while they were hiding out in the woods. I bet Erskin told him about it in case he wanted to fly in here. Which he did."

"You two figured it out pretty well," said Ollie in an admiring tone.

"There's only one problem," Frank replied. "We still don't know who he is!"

17 Flash Flood!

They stopped at the cabin, where Joe took the walkie-talkie and reported the incident to the rangers.

"We'll broadcast a warning to all law-enforcement agencies in the area," the officer on duty promised. "We'll stop anyone fitting this man's description. Were there any markings on the plane?"

"It didn't have any," Joe replied, "but it's a single-engine Cessna, propeller-driven. Seats four. And it's built for long-distance flying."

"That means it could have come from any number of states in the area," the ranger noted. "You have a good memory, especially considering the fight you had with the pilot."

Frank and Joe had been trained in memory

techniques by their father, and they had caught many criminals by rememberng important details.

When Joe finished his call to the rangers, he found Ollie sewing up his life jacket again. He finally snipped the cord with scissors and tested the repair by pulling at the tear.

"This vest is okay again," he declared. "It'll be watertight. Now let's go out and see what the others are doing."

Chet spoke up. "The cabin will be empty. Suppose that creep in the black beard comes back? There won't be anyone here to keep him from taking whatever he wants."

Joe shook his head. "He's a long way from here by now, and he won't return since he knows we spotted him."

"Besides, he must have been after the diamond ring," Frank theorized. "And he probably realized that Joe found it in the life jacket. So he has no reason to come back. It's lucky we were here to stop him when he showed up."

Suddenly, the buzzer on the walkie-talkie sounded. Ollie clicked the answer button.

"Waterway Rangers calling," said the voice on the other end. "There is a flash-flood warning for the Roaring River!"

"When will the flood reach us?" Ollie asked worriedly.

"Any minute now. Rain is falling heavily up near the headwaters, and it's pouring in from the hills. Get everybody off the river at once. This is an emergency. And take precautions against flooding."

Ollie turned off the walkie-talkie and relayed what the ranger had said. "There's a pile of sandbags behind the cabin," he told his friends. "We can build a dike along the river. But we don't have much time!"

Joe and Chet volunteered to help carry the sandbags.

"And I'll alert the guys on the river," Frank said. He ran out to the place where the expedition was practicing.

The raft was in the middle of the current, with the four members of the maintenance crew aboard. Tarn and Karl were working the oars, and had already noticed that the water was becoming rough.

Frank cupped his hands around his mouth and shouted as loudly as he could. "Come ashore! There's a flash-flood warning for this area. Get back before it hits the raft!"

"We read you!" Karl yelled. "We're coming in!" The current was becoming more turbulent. A wave caught the raft and hurled it forward. Karl expertly backpaddled and kept them from smashing into the bank. Then the crew scrambled ashore and Frank helped them carry the raft behind the cabin, which was the highest spot in the area.

"Let's not forget the canoe!" Karl said. "The rope might break and it'll float down the river!"

He and Frank returned to the bank, hauled the canoe out, and carried it up beside the raft, where the other canoes had been carried to safety. The rest of the crew were already lugging sandbags.

"Karl, you were great!" Frank said. "The raft could have been put out of commission if you hadn't backpaddled."

Karl grinned. "I've been practicing a lot. You know, I really wanted to be on one of the oars during the race. That's why I was so mad when you guys turned up. But it doesn't matter. The Fernandez expedition will run another river after this one. That's when I'll get my chance."

Frank and Karl joined in carrying the sandbags from the cabin to the river.

Chet strained under the weight. "These are as heavy as a ton of bricks!" he puffed.

"It's good exercise," Joe kidded. "It'll put you in great shape for the race! Keep going, Chet."

When they reached the river, they piled the sandbags along the bank. Soon a long line extended between the river and the cabin.

"That's all we have," Ollie said finally. "Let's hope they hold back the flood."

"The question is whether the water will rise over the sandbags," Joe commented as he surveyed the barricade.

"If it does, the cabin will be in danger," Frank predicted.

They all stood behind the barricade they had built and watched the river rise. A huge wave rippled downstream. Whirlpools churned along the banks, carrying away earth and rocks.

Inch by inch, the water rose, stopping suddenly near the top of the sandbags.

"We're safe!" Chet exulted.

Frank shook his head. "Don't be too sure. Another flash wave might be coming down from the hills."

Joe pointed upstream. "You're right, Frank. It's here already. Look!"

A second wave, larger than the first, roared down the river. The current in the middle moved faster, and a huge log floated past them.

The whirlpools near the banks became more turbulent as the water rose higher against the sandbags. When it reached the top, it spilled over.

The members of the expedition retreated as the area became flooded. They moved back step by step, avoiding the water rolling toward them over the ground. At last they had their backs to the cabin.

"We'd better get inside!" Joe cried. "We don't know how high it'll get!"

"We can climb up to the crossbeams beneath the roof," Frank seconded Joe's advice.

One by one, they piled into the little structure. Ollie slammed the door and locked it, while Frank and Joe carried a table from the center of the room and wedged it against the door.

"That'll hold it for a moment," Frank said.

Then everyone scrambled to the window to watch the flood. By now, water covered everything they could see, carrying bushes and saplings away. Rabbits and squirrels scampered toward higher ground.

A few minutes later, the water touched the lowest logs of the cabin and rose toward the door!

Ollie looked grim. "This is it," he warned. "Get that table from the corner and pile some chairs on it so we can climb to the rafters if necessary."

Tarn and Karl went for the furniture while Frank called the ranger headquarters on the walkie-talkie.

"Any report on the flash flood?" he asked anxiously.

"The crest upriver is diminishing," the officer reported. "The level of the water is beginning to fall."

"Then the flood is over?"

"Yes. All you have to do is dry out when the water recedes. Who is this?"

"Frank Hardy. I'm with the Fernandez expedition. Will the flood stop the race?"

"I don't think so. Brian Schmidt called in, too. His cabin is high enough above the river to be safe. How are things with you folks?"

"Everything's waterlogged except the cabin. We thought we were goners for a while."

"We'll send out a helicopter to see how you're doing," the ranger said, then the conversation ended.

Frank put the walkie-talkie down. "Not to worry," he announced. "The flood threat is over."

The water level was beginning to drop, and moved back from the cabin. The occupants cheered. Quickly they replaced the table and chairs, then Ollie opened the door and they went outside.

The grass sloshed under their feet as they followed the receding water to the river bank. There, the current was diminishing rapidly, and soon the river fell back into its normal channel.

Ollie said to the others, "Let's not just stand around. We have to make sure our equipment's okay. But first, let's carry the sandbags back behind the cabin."

Chet groaned. "I kinda like them right where they are. Why can't we leave them there?"

Frank chuckled. "Nice try, Chet. You know we have to leave this camp as clean as we found it."

The sandbags were lifted from the river bank and again piled behind the cabin. Then Ollie inspected the raft and pronounced it fit for the race. The boys carried it down to the river and left it where it could be pushed off directly into the water.

The sound of a helicopter echoed over the area. Then it landed on the airstrip near the cabin. Captain Lecore and two of his men came down the trail to the camp. Lecore introduced his companions as Sean Marcum and Joe Finch.

"How are you doing?" Lecore asked.

"Well, we didn't drown, Captain," Frank replied. "And we weren't swept away."

"But we had a ringside seat for the flood," Joe remarked. "Every fish in the river swam past our eyes."

Lecore laughed. "But what about your equipment? Is it ready for the race?"

Ollie nodded. "It sure is, Captain. Come on,

and I'll show you."

The rangers inspected the rubber raft. They punched its sides to make sure it was strong enough for a ride through the rapids. Next, they examined the oars for damage.

"Let's see the rest of your gear," Captain Lecore said. "And then I'll give you the rules for the race."

He led the way into the cabin where Ollie showed him the life jackets and crash helmets. The three rangers went over them carefully and put them down.

Lecore spoke to Ollie. "You meet the requirements of the Maine Boating Law, which says that every craft running a river must have at least one life-saving device for each person in it. Those life jackets will do fine. What do you intend to wear during the race?"

"Bathing trunks, wool sweaters, wool socks, and sneakers," Ollie told him.

"That's just what you need. Wool will keep you warm even when you get wet. And you'll sure get wet once you reach the white water! Remember—don't carry anything with you. No money, no wristwatches, nothing. Leave everything in the cabin except what you need for the race."

"How do we start?" Ollie inquired.

"You'll go down the river to meet the

Schmidt team. When both rafts are ready, Sean Marcum will fire the starting pistol. After that, you will be on your own until you go through the rapids and reach the finish line, which will be a tape tied to two pine trees on opposite sides of the river. Joe Finch and I will be there to register the winner and hand out the prize!"

Marcum added another point. "I've already warned Brian Schmidt about the danger of running the rapids here. You should know about it, too. We use a scale of one to six in rating rivers. One means you can float down if you want to. Six means the river is too tough to run at all. Well, the Roaring River rates a five. You can run it, but watch out! The water flows at ten miles per hour past the rocks at the most dangerous point. That's not much for a car, but it's murder for a rubber raft!"

"If one of you falls overboard and can't get back," Finch said, "I guess you know to float downstream feet first. That way you won't get hurt much if you hit a rock. A helicopter will be circling over the river and will pick you up."

As the rangers rose to go, Lecore turned to Joe with a solemn expression.

"By the way," he said, "we have no report on the fugitive in disguise you described to our man at headquarters, or on the unmarked plane he was flying. He must have gotten away."

18 Running the Rapids

In the morning, all the members of the expedition went through the final practice for the race the next day. Frank and Joe showed they could handle the raft expertly while Ollie and Chet were on the oars.

At one point, the tip of Chet's oar skimmed the surface of the river, throwing a fine spray into the air. The force of his stroke caused the chubby boy to lose his balance and he fell backward off his seat.

"Chet, you just caught a crab!" Joe laughed. "That's what they say when you can't find the water with your oar."

Chet blushed as he scrambled back onto his

seat. "I'd rather catch a crab in the bay with a net," he grumbled. "The oar slipped on me, that's all."

"Don't worry," Ollie said. "Everybody catches a crab once in a while."

The boys spent a good part of the day studying the rapids. When they came back, Ollie said, "We have everything down pat. Let's go over our strategy now. We need to get our signals straight."

They discussed the best way to outrun Brian Schmidt and his crew.

"It'll be a hard race," Ollie predicted. "They know how to run through white water."

"And they're confident they can take us," Frank added. "That's what they told Joe and me when we went over there."

"We can't let those guys get the jump on us," Chet interjected. "We know the race will begin in easy water above the rapids. That's where we should grab the lead and hold it if we can."

Frank agreed. "There are two stretches of rapids separated by an open area, remember? If we're ahead when we reach the first white water, we may be able to stay ahead for good."

Ollie nodded. "We'll go full steam from the moment we hear the starter's pistol."

"And we'll cheer you on," Karl declared,

speaking for the maintenance crew.

That evening the young people listened to music on a cassette Ollie had brought. Afterward they went to bed, filled with thoughts about the next day's adventure on the Roaring River.

Chet dreamed that he was going over Niagara Falls in a raft. He looked down the steep cataract of tumbling water and saw the swirling whirlpool far below. With a cry of panic, he fell toward it!

Catching his breath, he woke up. It took him a moment to realize where he was. "Boy, I hope we don't have to run a waterfall tomorrow!" he thought, then turned over and went back to sleep.

The members of the expedition were up early the following morning. After a quick breakfast, they donned their life jackets and crash helmets.

The clatter of a ranger helicopter settling down on the airstrip told them that Sean Marcum was on his way. He arrived shortly afterward and accompanied them to the river.

"I'll ride with you down to the point where the race begins," he said. "There we'll meet Brian Schmidt's raft. Meanwhile, your maintenance people will go to the finish line in the helicopter I came in. It's waiting on the airstrip."

The crew left to catch the helicopter. Joe climbed aboard the raft and took his place in the bow, where he would serve as lookout. Ollie and Chet followed him to their seats at the oars. Sean Marcum came next, and then Frank, who untied the rope holding the raft. He pushed against the bank with his oar, and they moved out into the middle of the river, heading downstream at a rapid pace until they saw the Schmidt raft tied to the shore.

Frank moved beside it. Sean Marcum went ashore and inspected the equipment of the rival team. "You're ready, too," he informed Brian. Then he called out: "The race can begin! Both crews, take your positions in the middle of the river!"

As the rafts moved away from the bank, the crews called out good-naturedly to one another.

"Okay, fellows, remember what I said!" Ormsby cried. "We'll beat you with our eyes shut!"

"No way!" Frank retorted. "We're in this race to win! You should have stayed in your cabin!"

Schmidt laughed. "Not on your life. We'll pick up the prize!"

Marcum shouted from the bank. "Okay, line

up the rafts! Fernandez on the right, Schmidt on the left. Leave enough space so your oars don't collide!"

When the rafts were properly aligned in the swiftly flowing current, the ranger drew his starter's pistol from its holster and pointed it high over his head. The crews poised tensely for the sound of the shot.

Bang! The blank exploded in the chamber, and the oars hit the water as the rafts jolted foreward.

The oarsmen pulled strenuously, and the contestants moved rapidly down the river. They ran neck and neck for a couple of hundred yards, then the Fernandez raft pulled ahead.

Joe called out directions to take advantage of the fastest-moving water in the center of the current. Frank steered by letting his oar trail off the stern and shifting it from side to side. Ollie and Chet rhythmically lifted their oars and dipped them into the water.

They had a good lead on Schmidt when they heard the roar of the first rapids. Now the river became rough, as they headed directly toward a group of massive boulders.

"Frank, bear to the left!" Joe shouted. "It's the only safe route!"

Frank shifted his oar. The raft turned and

they skirted the boulders. The passage was so narrow that Ollie shipped his oar while Chet rowed. Frank kept on course by skillful steering. Once they were past the boulders, Ollie went back to rowing.

Now they were in the middle of the white water, and the raft bounced up and down furiously. An especially heavy wave struck a rock and recoiled with the current. Before the crew could do anything, the wave carried them between two submerged boulders. Ollie and Chet barely had time to ship their oars when the raft became caught between the rocks and jarred to a stop.

"We have to back up!" Joe called. He picked up a paddle he had for such emergencies and pushed against the rocks in front of them. Ollie and Chet did the same on either side with their oars. Released from the trap, the raft moved backward into the white water.

The maneuver had taken so much time that Brian Schmidt and his crew managed to pass them, shouting gibes about expert river runners who get caught in the rapids.

"They were able to avoid the rocks because we ran into them!" Frank muttered. "How lucky can they get?"

The Fernandez raft took up the pursuit.

Reaching the end of the first white water, they saw Brian Schmidt moving down another wide space in the river. Yard by yard, Frank, Joe, Chet and Ollie narrowed the gap. Soon they were abreast of the rival crew. Taking the lead again, they plunged into the second rapids, which were worse than the first.

Here the Roaring River made a steep descent, and the current ran twice as fast as before. The raft careened from side to side. It grazed boulders and slid over rocks where the water became shallow. Hurtling into a deep whirlpool, it was lifted up by the turbulent water and turned completely around! The crew felt their hearts skip a beat and they gasped for breath!

They slammed down into the water and then bounced like a cork, drenched to the skin. But Ollie and Chet did not miss a beat as they resumed rowing. Joe wiped the spray from his eyes and peered intently into the water for rocks and shallows. Frank strained his ears to hear Joe's directions over the loud roar.

"Slightly to the left," Joe shouted.

They slid over a drop in the riverbed. The bow slammed into the water and rose out of it again. Huge waves broke over all those on board, and the raft shuddered under the impact.

Frank wondered if they could survive the

pounding—until they settled down in the water and rode the current again.

But they barely straightened out when they came to another sudden descent. This time they hit with such force that Chet dropped his oar into the water. He stood up and leaned over the side of the raft to retrieve it. However, the oar escaped his grasp. He reached farther out into the river.

"Chet! Sit down!" Frank yelled.

A split-second later an enormous wave washed over them and Chet lost his balance! With a sharp cry, he fell overboard into the raging rapids, and went under in a torrent of white foam!

Carried upward by his life jacket, Chet bobbed back to the surface. As he flailed around in the water, he felt his hand close around his oar. The raft was just passing him when Frank reached out and got hold of Chet's life vest. Chet threw one arm over the edge of the raft, and clung to the oar with the other hand. At that moment, the current threw them against a boulder, and his weight brought the raft to a halt.

Frank and Ollie pulled Chet inside the raft. Without a word, he took his seat, steadied his oar in the water, and began to row. But so much time had been lost that the Schmidt expedition caught up and took the lead again.

"Good-bye!" Ormsby yelled. "We'll see you later—at the finish line!"

"You'll see us sooner than that!" Joe replied. "Don't get in our way when we come through!"

The Schmidt crew rounded a curve in the river and disappeared. Ollie and his companions set out after them at top speed. Taking the bend themselves, they saw their rivals close to the end of the rapids.

Ollie and Chet rowed as fast as they could. Joe warned of the rocks in front, and Frank steered skillfully away from them. The raft zigzagged through the last of the rapids and raced into the broad, lower end of the river. Schmidt was still a hundred yards ahead.

"Do you think we can catch them?" Chet puffed as he lifted his oar for another stroke.

"We've got a mile to go," Frank said grimly. "And we'd better!"

Ollie and Chet were wielding their oars at top speed, and their raft gained on the leader. Brian Schmidt looked back. "We've got to go faster!" he cried. "They're coming up on us!"

The two crews put everything into their effort to win the race.

Joe noticed that the current was swiftest to

the right of the raft. "Bear to the right!" he called back.

Frank steered expertly, and they picked up speed. Now the finish line was in sight. A long ribbon crossed the water between two trees near the place where the Roaring River emptied into the Allagash. The two rangers, Lecore and Marcum, stood on one bank, along with the maintenance crews for both rafts. Everyone began to cheer as the contestants came in sight.

The Schmidt crew struggled to keep the lead. But Ollie and his friends steadily closed the gap and drew even. It was a nip-and-tuck battle until the finish line was only yards away.

Joe kept an eagle eye on the fastest part of the current and directed Frank accordingly. With a last burst of effort, Ollie and Chet propelled their raft ahead. It broke the ribbon, and won the race by a nose!

19 Frank Finds the Loot

There were loud cheers from the spectators on the river bank as the two crews stopped their rafts. They shipped their oars and, still out of breath, floated side by side in the water. The members leaned over and shook hands, congratulating one another.

"Ollie, you beat us fair and square," Brian Schmidt admitted. "You deserve the prize."

Ormsby added his compliments. "You won in spite of the two accidents you had. We never had a crew catch up with us under those circumstances!"

"Thanks, fellows," Ollie replied. "You ran a great race, too."

Then the young people rowed to the river

bank and clambered ashore. Captain Lecore and Joe Finch greeted them, while the maintenance crews took charge of the rafts, the life jackets, and the crash helmets.

Finch summoned the Schmidt team around him. "Even though you didn't win, you deserve credit for running the rapids of the Roaring River," the ranger declared. "We therefore have decided to award a second prize." He handed Brian a check for $2,500.

"Wow!" Brian exclaimed, and slapped hands with his happy crew. "That's great, sir! We'll use this money for our next expedition."

"Where will you go?" Joe Finch asked.

"We were considering the Feather River in California," Brian replied. "We can't wait to see Devil Canyon and the Feather Falls."

"Well, good luck to you. Now, Ollie, here's the first prize for you boys," Finch went on. "You won five thousand dollars and a special citation from the state of Maine. It's signed by the governor."

He drew a parchment from his pocket and unrolled it. The young people could see the painted sketch of a raft riding through white water. Beneath it were printed the words: FIRST TO RUN THE RAPIDS OF THE ROARING RIVER IN THE ALLAGASH WILDERNESS WATERWAY.

A blank space was left for the names of the winning crew. The ranger looked around. "I need something to write on. A board, or a life jacket, or whatever you can find that's hard enough."

Chet grinned. "You can use me for a desk," he said.

Turning around, he leaned over with his hands on his knees, offering his broad back as a writing board. Laughing, Joe Finch placed the parchment between Chet's shoulders. Frank held the top corners, Joe the bottom, and the ranger took out his pen.

He filled in the blank space on the citation with the names: OLLIE FERNANDEZ, FRANK HARDY, JOE HARDY, CHET MORTON.

Chet straightened up, as Joe Finch handed the parchment to Ollie. "What's next for you fellows?" he inquired.

"We're heading for Georgia," Ollie responded, "where we want to run the Painted Rock Rapids."

"Not us, Ollie," Frank told him. "We're on our way back home to Bayport."

"You don't need us anyway," Joe pointed out. "Karl and the others are more than ready to crew."

"Well, you three were a big help this time," Ollie said. "We couldn't have done it without you."

"Maybe Chet wants to go to Georgia with you," Joe remarked jokingly.

"Not me!" Chet said hastily. "The one time I got dunked was enough for me, and I decided to get another hobby—a dry one!"

Everyone laughed, then Captain Lecore, who had been standing quietly next to Joe Finch while the ranger handed out the prizes, spoke up.

"Now, fellows, since it's impossible for you to row up the rapids, a helicopter will take all of you to the airstrip near the Fernandez cabin. The Schmidt crew can get back to their camp from there by floating down the river. So please deflate your rafts, carry the rest of your gear, and come along with me."

He led the way to a small airstrip about three hundred yards back in the woods. The deflated rafts, oars, life jackets, and crash helmets were stowed aboard the chopper, and the crews got in. Minutes later they landed upriver.

"We'll be back in the morning," Captain Lecore announced. "Pickup trucks will take the crews and their equipment out. Frank and Joe

Hardy, Chet Morton—you'll go by helicopter. We'll leave you at the airfield south of the waterway, where you can catch a plane for Bayport."

A few moments later the chopper flew off, and the crews carried their gear down the trail to Ollie's cabin.

"Brian, there's no need to leave yet," Ollie said. "Have some chow with us first."

The Schmidt crew cheered, and their leader gladly accepted the invitation.

They all showered and changed into dry clothes. "We found some shirts and jeans when we got here," Ollie said to Ormsby. "You guys might as well take them."

"Thanks," Ormsby replied. "It's no fun putting on wet clothes again, that's for sure."

Frank made hamburgers on the grill, while Joe and Chet got cases of cold soda from the kitchen. They were all so hungry that the food quickly disappeared.

Then Karl brought out his guitar, and Tarn started to play his harmonica. Elated by the race and the prize money they had won, the young people sang their favorite songs and clapped hands to the rhythm of the music.

Finally they all went down to the river, where Schmidt's maintenance crew inflated their raft. There were handshakes all around, then Brian and his friends finally floated out of sight.

The following morning the members of the Fernandez expedition packed their gear and cleaned the cabin until it was spotless. They brought their canoes from the river, then scouted around the entire area, picking up any debris they could find.

"Okay, the cabin's shipshape for the next occupants," Ollie judged. "I wonder who they'll be."

"Could be backpackers," Joe suggested. "There's plenty of forest to hike in."

"Or river runners," Frank put in, "now that we've shown it's possible to navigate these rapids."

"Well, I hope the next raft has pros as good as you fellows." Ollie grinned.

The rangers arrived a half hour later. Ollie Fernandez and his friends said good-bye, stowed their equipment and canoes aboard the pickup, and departed.

"We're ready to go, but we didn't solve the mystery," Joe lamented. "We didn't find the loot from the bank robbery."

"You did as much as you could when you located the thieves in the woods," Captain Lecore said, "and you did recover the stolen diamond ring. Well, the helicopter's waiting. We might as well fly out."

They were on the way to the airstrip, when Frank suddenly knew what had been nagging at him all along.

"Wait a minute, Captain," he said. "Let's go back to the cabin. I just have this gut feeling that the solution to this mystery is in there somehow."

Lecore shrugged. "You boys cleaned the place thoroughly. I can't imagine you missed anything."

"Well, we didn't really look for hiding places, like in the wall or in the floor," Frank said. "But it seems to me the thieves must have had another reason to want to get rid of the Fernandez expedition—besides retrieving the life jackets. Maybe they hid the loot in the cabin!"

"What?" Joe cried out. "Why would they hide it in a place occupied by someone else?"

"I don't know, but I think it's worth another look, anyway."

The group returned to the camp and Frank said, "Why don't we split up and search systematically, room by room. Let's check the walls, the floor, around the windows, in the closets, and so on. I'll start in the bedroom."

He got down on his knees and ran his hands

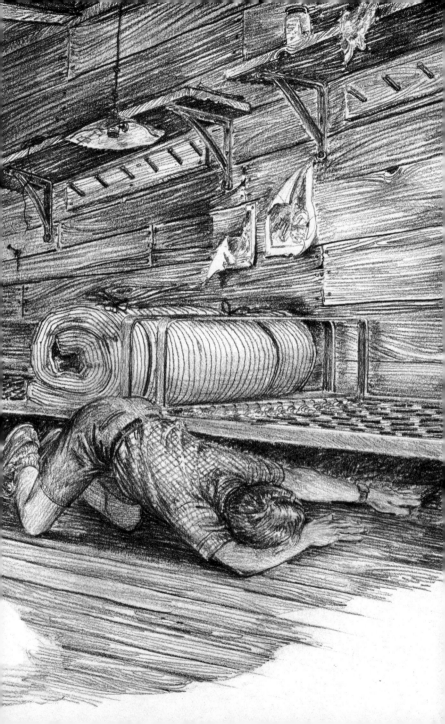

across the floorboards under the first bunk. There was nothing. He repeated the search under the next bunk, but again it was in vain.

Continuing down the line in the same way, he finally came to the last bunk, the one he had slept in.

Thrusting his arm beneath it, he patted around across the floorboards. Next to the wall, he felt one give a little. He pressed his fingers into the crevices on either side and pulled upward. The board came out! Frank placed it to one side and pushed his hand into the space underneath. His fingers closed around a handle!

With a loud yell, he drew out a black brief-case! The others crowded around as Frank laid the case flat on the table and sprang the catches on both sides with his thumbs. The case flew open.

Everyone gaped in surprise. "The stolen money!" Captain Lecore said in awe. "You found it!"

The briefcase was lined with thousand-dollar bills.

"There's the million dollars the crooks took from the bank," Joe gasped.

The bills were in packages held together by rubber bands. Frank lifted them out and stacked them on the table. At the bottom, he found several documents, which he held up for everyone to see.

"These are the securities the gang stole from the bank," he cried triumphantly.

Captain Lecore took the documents, looked them over, and handed them back. "You're right, Frank. These belong to a foreign government. The Treasury Department will be glad to have them back!"

"I still can't figure out why the gang would hide this stuff here," Chet spoke up. "How did they get into this place with Ollie's expedition using it?"

Captain Lecore held up his hand. "It's only a guess, but this is what I think happened. The thieves must have arrived before Ollie and his people and moved into the cabin, thinking it was free for them to use since no one else was around."

Frank was thoughtful. "I bet that's right. When Black told the gang about the diamond ring in the life vest, I suppose they decided to come up to Maine. A cabin in the woods would be as good a hideout as any, and they had a chance to get the ring back. They knew Ollie was going to run the rapids here—"

"But Ollie ordered the life jackets a day after

the robbery," Joe put in. "That means he was already here—"

"No, we weren't," Ollie put in. "I ordered them from home on the second, and we came up on the third. But I knew it would take a while before they'd be delivered, so I had them shipped to Maine."

"That explains it!" Frank said triumphantly. "The gang thought Ollie was here already, camping out somewhere. They found the empty cabin and moved in, not realizing that Ollie had rented it and would be coming up the next day!"

"But then how come Ollie and his friends didn't find the gang here when they arrived?" Chet asked.

"The thieves probably heard the helicopter land and saw the expedition coming down from the airstrip," Frank said. "They realized that they were headed for the cabin, so they took off in a hurry. In such a hurry, as a matter of fact, that they didn't have time to take the loot!"

"Come to think of it," Ollie said, "when we got here, we found some clothes and stuff around. We thought the previous tenants had left them—that's how we had those extra jeans and shirts we gave to Brian and his crew."

"I'm sure that's what happened," Captain

Lecore declared. "You boys solved the mystery after all. Congratulations!"

"Not quite," Frank said soberly. "We still have to figure out who has been masterminding this whole scheme!"

20 Breaking the Code

Frank put the documents back into the brief-case and stacked the packages of thousand-dollar bills on top of them. Then he snapped it shut.

"Instead of going to Bayport," he said, "I think we should fly straight to Washington and return this and the diamond ring to the bank."

Captain Lecore nodded. "That's a very good idea. I'll notify the manager and tell him you're on your way."

The group walked from the cabin to the airstrip for the helicopter ride out. The chopper swung up over the trees and headed south over the Allagash Wilderness Waterway, passing the falls. Even at their height, they could see the force of the water hurtling down at a forty-degree angle.

Chet gulped. "Boy, I'm glad we didn't run *those* rapids!"

Lecore laughed. "Nobody runs that stretch of the river, Chet. That's not rapids down there. That's a waterfall."

The flight continued over the lakes and streams of the waterway, and soon landed at the airfield beyond the lower end. Frank, Joe, and Chet stepped down onto the runway.

Captain Lecore called good-bye to them. "You'll all receive copies of the citation for running the Roaring River," he said. "So will the maintenance crew of the Fernandez expedition. The original will be on display at the Waterway Rangers Headquarters. Look for it the next time you're up here."

"We sure will, Captain," Frank replied. "We do hope to return soon."

The chopper took off, and the boys went to catch a connecting flight. However, only two seats were available on the plane to Washington.

"Well, instead of waiting for the next flight," Chet said, "why don't you two go ahead. You don't really need me anymore now, so I'll head home."

"Good idea," Joe said, and the friends separated. When the Hardys arrived in Washington, they took a taxi to the Grandison Hotel. Joe had the diamond ring in his pocket as they mounted the front steps. Frank was carrying the brief-case.

Joe went through the revolving door. Frank was about to follow when he heard footsteps running up behind him. Startled, he whirled around and saw a man with black hair, a black mustache, and a black beard. The man was wearing heavily tinted glasses. In a flash, he wrenched the briefcase from Frank's hand and turned to flee!

Frank took a flying leap through the air. He seized the thief around the shoulders and pushed him down the steps, where both of them crashed in a heap. The case fell onto the sidewalk, and the cover sprang open. Packages of thousand-dollar bills spilled out!

Frank wrestled with the man and almost had him pinned down, when his opponent jerked to the left and broke free. He jumped nimbly to his feet and ran away.

Meanwhile, a crowd had gathered around the money on the sidewalk. Frank knew he could not follow the man and leave thousand-dollar bills on the street, so he hurried to the spot and collected the money. When he had finished, the man with the black beard had vanished.

By this time, Joe had come out of the hotel. "What happened?" he asked. "I was talking to Ken Bulow when I realized you weren't behind me."

"Our friend Blackbeard almost took off with the briefcase," Frank said, and brushed the dirt off his pants. "We drew quite a crowd. Let's get out of here before people begin to ask questions."

Quickly he walked into the hotel lobby, Joe at his side. The desk clerk was just finishing with a guest.

"Hi, Ken," Frank greeted him. "Have you seen a man with black hair, a black mustache, and a black beard around here?"

"He also wears tinted spectacles," Joe added. "They're so dark you can't see his eyes."

Bulow shook his head. "Is he a friend of yours?"

"No," Joe replied. "He's involved in the case our father's working on."

Ken shrugged. "Sorry, I haven't seen anyone fitting that description." Then he grinned. "Maybe Mr. Harper has. He's in your old room. Go on up, and this time I won't follow you."

The boys thanked the clerk, and a few minutes later were knocking on the door of number 15.

Mr. Hardy let them in and welcomed them

back to Washington. "I heard you boys helped put Wolf Erskin and his gang behind bars," he said.

"We did more than that!" Joe said. "We found the money and the securities in our cabin in Maine. We have it right here in this briefcase. And we have the diamond ring, too."

"What!" Mr. Hardy was flabbergasted. "Tell me all about it."

The boys took turns reporting what had happened during their stay up north. "By the way," Frank concluded, "we also won the white-water race on the rapids. Ollie got a check for five thousand dollars, and is he excited!"

Mr. Hardy looked proudly at his sons. "I can't keep up with you supersleuths anymore," he said. "You really did a great job!"

"Don't say that yet," Frank replied. "We stumbled on the gang by sheer accident. And we still haven't found out who the director is. We don't have a clue."

"We assume he's the guy in the black-beard disguise who showed up in Maine before we left, and just now met us at the hotel door to steal the money. But he didn't get away with it," Joe said.

"We'll return the documents and the money to Mr. Barcross personally," Mr. Hardy announced. "I'll call him right now and ask him to come over in a security van. I'd rather not chance leaving the hotel with that briefcase unprotected." He phoned the bank manager, and twenty minutes later there was a knock on the door. Mr. Hardy opened it and Barcross entered.

He was puffing and mopping his face with a handkerchief. He took off his coat and draped it over a chair. "It's hot today," he said. "Besides, I'm so excited that you boys brought back everything stolen from my bank!"

Frank gave him the briefcase. Joe took the diamond ring from his pocket and handed it over. Barcross accepted both with expressions of gratitude.

"Did you find out who the director is?" the bank manager asked anxiously.

Frank shook his head. "He's the one person we haven't identified."

"That's too bad. I'm afraid he may rob the bank again! I won't feel safe till he's in jail!"

Joe took from his pocket the architect's diagram he had found at the entrance to the tunnel in the basement of The Sports Center. He spread it out on the table and pointed to the + – sign.

"This is the only clue we have," he declared. "We know those symbols that look like a plus and minus sign are the code to our man. That's how he signed orders to his gang. But we don't know what the symbols mean."

Barcross shook his head. "If you ask me, those marks are the work of a mad mathematician!"

Frank was looking at the symbols. Something had just rung a bell in his mind, but he couldn't put his finger on it. He frowned. Then, suddenly, it was all clear to him.

"Mr. Barcross," he said. "You had no way of knowing that the man behind this scheme calls himself the ' director.' It's a rather unusual title for a gang boss, and we didn't hear it mentioned until we overheard the gang in the Maine woods."

Barcross flushed. "Well, being in banking, it's a very familiar title to me—"

"That's right," Frank went on. "And those symbols are not mathematical signs either. They don't stand for plus and minus. They represent a *cross* and a *bar*. Reverse them, and they read Barcross!"

The bank manager was so stunned that he stood frozen to the spot. Finally he managed to collect himself. "You're crazy!" he cried. "You can't pin that code on me. You have no proof!"

"I think we have more proof than we need," Joe said. While Frank was speaking, Joe had eyed the man's jacket that was draped over the chair. Something black was sticking out of one pocket.

Joe walked over to it and pulled out a black wig. Then he reached into the other pocket and retrieved a false mustache and beard. A search of the inside pocket produced a pair of tinted glasses!

Joe held them up in the air. "This is your disguise," he said to Barcross. "You wore it to the Library of Congress when you copied the architect's diagram. You wore it to the Roaring River when you looked at us through the cabin window, and I chased you to the plane you used to escape. And you wore it just now outside the hotel when you tried to get the briefcase away from Frank!"

"You figured you'd escape with the securities," Frank took up the story, "fly abroad, and sell them to your contact. When that failed, you decided to keep your appointment here with us. But you didn't have a chance to ditch your disguise. So, you stuffed it into your pockets."

Barcross said nothing.

Frank continued with the accusation. "As the head of the bank, you were able to plan the robbery. You knew about the tunnel and told Wolf Erskin how to defuse the bank's alarm system. And you had an accomplice, Bill Black, in The Sports Center. He showed Erskin how to get in there. Later, he shadowed us because you told him we were investigating the robbery."

Barcross still said nothing.

"By the way," Joe added, "I think Black will talk when he knows we've retrieved the loot. He's not the type to keep quiet when there's nothing in it for him."

The bank manager saw what Joe was getting at, and feeling defeated, he confessed that the Hardys were right.

"When we moved, I was looking at plans of the bank building in the Library of Congress," he said. "I stumbled on the diagram showing the tunnel and realized that someone could get through the passage and rob the bank. So, I went back in disguise and made a copy for Wolf Erskin."

"Erskin claims he doesn't know your identity," Joe observed.

"He's right about that," Barcross affirmed. "I wore my disguise when I persuaded him to pull off the heist. Earl Majors knew who I was because we went to school together years ago. He came down to Washington and we arranged for him to be my go-between with the gang. He recommended Erskin for the job, by the way."

Barcross wearily sat down in a chair. "I needed the money," he continued, "because I had made some bad investments of my own—"

"With the bank's funds," Frank put in.

Barcross nodded. "I—I just didn't know what to do."

"So you staged a robbery of your own bank," Joe concluded. "Then your gang went to Maine to retrieve the diamond ring and to hide out until you could dispose of the securities."

Barcross nodded. "Majors was familiar with the territory up there and met them. He didn't know Fernandez had rented the cabin, so they moved in—but had to take off in a hurry when he and his crew arrived. We thought we could just wait until the river race was over, but I found a buyer for the securities and I needed the briefcase."

Mr. Hardy nodded.

"But before your people could get the documents back, they were arrested. You were told by the authorities, since *you* were the bank manager. So you flew to the Roaring River yourself. You knew the briefcase was in the cabin, and there was nobody left to retrieve it for you."

"That's correct," Barcross said. "First I checked that the Fernandez raft was out on the river. I thought all the boys were practicing for the race. I was startled when I looked through the window and saw four people inside, including your sons."

"Then I chased you to the plane in the glade," Joe commented. "But I didn't win our wrestling match. Not after you threw dirt in my eyes."

Mr. Hardy spoke sternly. "I suppose the rangers notified you that the boys were coming to Washington with the money and the securities. So you waited near the Grandison Hotel in your disguise and attacked Frank, almost getting away with the briefcase after all."

Barcross shrugged. "Almost."

Mr. Hardy called the police. After the bank manager had been taken into custody, the detective drove to the police to make his report, while Frank and Joe went to tell Mr. Michaels what had happened. On the way, Frank felt a bit low, as he usually did at the end of a mystery. The future looked unexciting to him because he had no idea that soon they would have an adventure in the Vermont woods, called *The Demon's Den*.

At The Sports Center, they found Mr. Michaels in his office.

"You say Bill Black joined the gang in Maine!" he exclaimed. "I was wondering where he went. You boys were right on target to consider him a suspect."

Frank chuckled. "Mr. Michaels, we considered *you* a suspect for a while."

Michaels looked startled. "Me?"

"Yes. You seemed very nervous when we mentioned white-water rafting."

"That's because of my nephew. You see, a few days before you came to see me, I learned that he had been hurt while running the rapids somewhere out West. When you told me that you were interested in white-water rafting, I thought of Jeffrey. He's just about your age—"

Mr. Michael's voice trailed off, then he continued. "The only other time that I remember discussing rafting with you was at the library after I had read up on the sport."

Frank and Joe didn't know what to say. "We—we're sorry," Frank stammered. "If you had told us then—"

"I had no reason to," Mr. Michaels replied. "Anyway, I don't want to spoil it for you. You just did such a fine job solving this mystery that you deserve a reward. Pick out anything in my store, and it's yours!"

Frank and Joe smiled. "How about one of those nice, lightweight life jackets?" Joe suggested. "And if it happens to have a diamond ring in it, we wouldn't mind, either!"